ADRIFT IN THE GULF STREAM

Marvin Cook

Sequel to *Across Florida Straits*

The author thanks, first and foremost, Lee Cook for proofing, editing and encouragement. Test readers of the draft provided valuable comments and suggestions that are most appreciated. Thank you to Sue and Joe Doker, Frank and Pat Hankins, Doug Bailey, Maxine Glenn, Heather Massey French, and Pete and Pam Scalco.

Marvin Cook has traveled throughout the United States and Caribbean working to connect people to natural and cultural history at parks, museums, and wildlife refuges. Fiction has liberated his imagination, allowing him to invent characters maneuvering through dramatic circumstances in interesting places. When not writing or painting Florida and Maine landscapes, Cook sails the coast of Florida and spends summers aboard a boat in Downeast Maine with his wife, Lee.

Other books by Marvin Cook

Across Florida Straits
From Cuba to Key West

Houseboat Hermit
of the Everglades

Can't Outrun the Past
Not a Secret if You Tell Anyone

They all called him PINKY

Dystopian Paradise

Blue Goose Passport

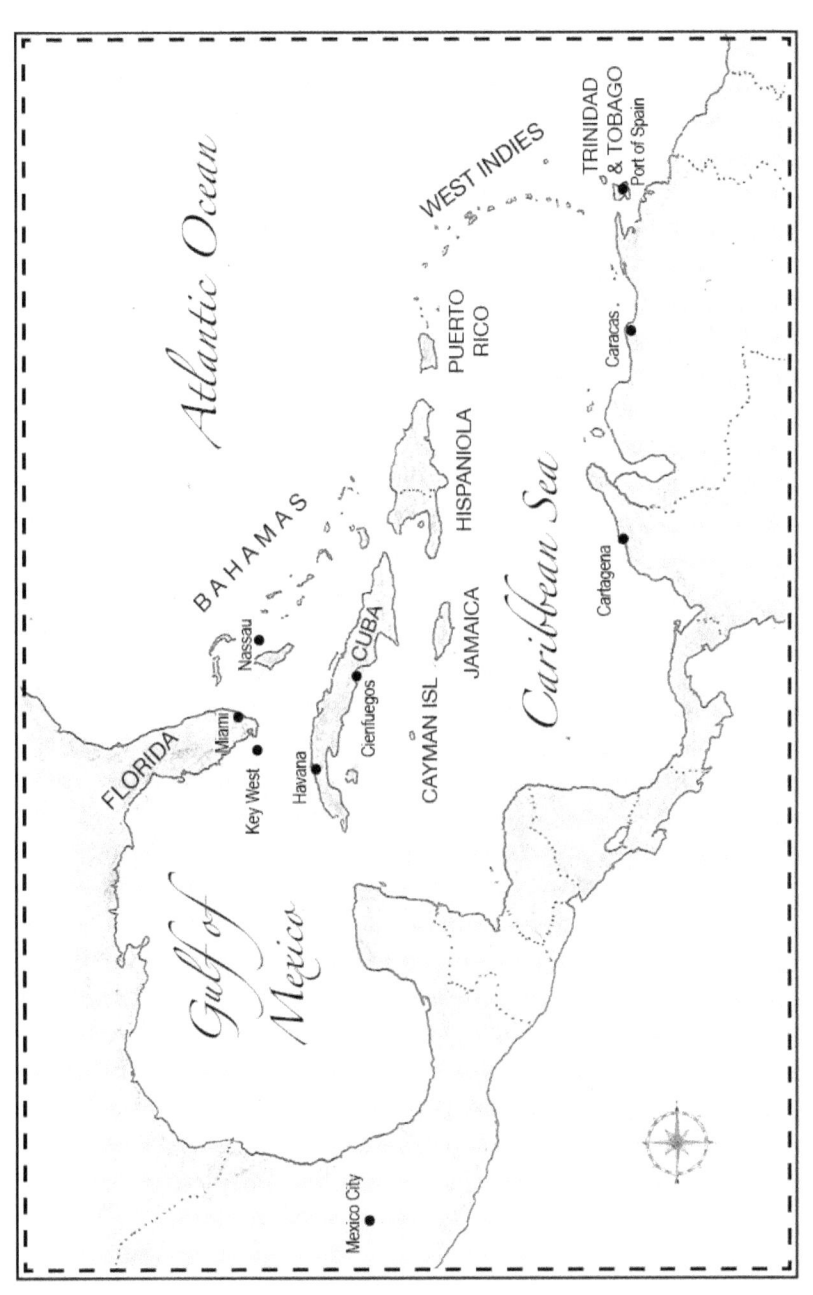

ONE

Matvey was alone in the ocean. Rising to the crest of a rolling swell he could barely make out a small speck in the distance. *La Luna Grande* was steaming away.

He felt relieved, realizing the men had given up their search for him. Now, he could catch his breath, thankful that he was alive. When he was on the boat, he felt certain the enraged captain was going to slit his throat.

Now, his demon was the ocean and its denizens. In the Gulf Stream somewhere between Havana and Key West, he was all on his own. At least the water was warm and he could float.

He searched the horizon until he could no longer see *La Luna Grande*. Twirling around in a circle while treading water, he scanned the expanse for any other boat. Yes, he was alone. That was a good thing and a bad thing. It was good that *La Luna Grande* was gone, but on the other hand, there were no other boats to rescue him. He was floating in the sea, maybe a hundred miles from land.

As he drifted, time was as fluid as the salt water. Matvey couldn't tell how long it had been since he had been held captive on the boat. Was it moments ago or maybe it had been hours? The sun was burning his skin. The water stung his eyes as he squinted to search for help in the distance. As he floated, he replayed his escape in his mind.

Matvey remembered that the captain had him in his grasp with a filet knife pressing against his neck. The other two men on the boat were leaning on the side of the cabin, smugly watching and waiting to see what Captain Alvero would do. Detective Costa and Agent Fernández had told him their job had been to snatch him in Key West and bring him bring him back to Cuba to stand trial for his crimes against the government. When Captain Alvero looked over to Costa and Fernández for permission to kill him, they replied that they did not care. They told Alvero, "You are the captain. The sea is your jurisdiction, not ours. We will return to Cuba, with either a thief of antiquities or a murderer of a thief."

When Captain Alvero heard this, he loosened his grip on Matvey's throat for just a moment. At that instant, sensing the filet knife was no longer poking his neck, Matvey lunged over the transom, bouncing off the boat's swim platform and flopping into the water.

As Matvey kicked away from the boat, he saw Alvero hurry up the tuna tower ladder to restart the engines and steer the boat to either retrieve him or run him over. Costa and Fernández raced to the boat's transom in a panic. He heard the captain shout, "If I run over him it will be an accident, not murder!"

Matvey used the confusion created when he went overboard to dive underwater and swim toward the bow of the boat. Once under the bow, he leaped as far out of the water as he could, grabbing the bow eye on the hull. He then leveraged himself to reach up and hang on the brace for the anchor platform. He hung there on his perch for what seemed like hours. *La Luna Grande* slowly motored in circles, searching for the escaped captive.

Matvey's arms ached with fatigue. He focused on the sleek, pointed hull, the rusty tip of the large anchor hanging above him, and the rippling of the waters as the boat maneuvered through the rolling seas. The ocean rose and fell as the boat slowly plodded through the swells while the captain looked for him in the sea. Matvey could hear the men on the boat shouting at one another.

He heard one man come to the bow. He could see the man's shadow on the water, but could not tell which of the men it was. Then, he heard someone shout, "Is that him over there?" The man retreated to the stern, as the boat turned in a new direction.

"No! Shit! It's just a lobster trap float."

G2 Agent Oscar Fernández, Detective Inspector Carlos Costa, and Captain Alvero Camilo Marin-Zayas were stunned that they had lost their prisoner. They were arguing about how to find and retrieve him in the waves. The seas were not rough; he should have been easy to find unless he had sunk into the depths of the Florida Straits. The captain continued slowly patrolling in a circle search pattern for another half hour before giving up.

Matvey heard Captain Alvero yell to the other two, "He must have been taken by the sea and joined my grandson. He is the reason my grandson drowned!"

Matvey heard one of the men exclaim, "Well, it looks like this was an accident at sea. I guess that means we do not have to report that you murdered our prisoner!"

Hearing the engines rumble louder as Alvero slowly throttled up to increase speed, Matvey let go of the anchor platform brace and dropped into the water. He dove as deep as he could, mustering all of his strength. He knew he needed to avoid the propellers and being seen as the boat sped over top of him. He felt the wash of the props as he exited under the stern. He was hoping beyond hope that no one saw him as he landed in the water. In the foaming wake, he was not as visible as he would have been on a flat calm day. During his brief glimpse before diving, he noticed all three men were facing forward. Did that mean they had given up looking for him? Matvey wasn't taking any chances that he might be seen. He quickly grabbed a breath of air and dove down underwater to wait.

Repeating his pattern of surfacing to breathe and quickly diving again, he heard the muffled sounds of *La Luna Grande's* engines. When he could no longer hear the sound while underwater, he surfaced longer to look around. In the far distance, he saw the boat up on a plane, headed off, away from him, likely back to Havana. Now that his pursuers were far enough away, he could begin to assess his situation. He was breathing heavily so he turned onto his back and floated to rest.

As Matvey floated and time passed, to distract himself from the increasing fear that he might die at sea and the terror that he would be attacked by sharks, he made up games in his head, like counting backward, in English, from 100. Soon, the sun beating down and the gentle roll of the ocean began to mesmerize him and he started hallucinating, remembering his past and how he got into this situation.

TWO

General Rodolfo Diego met the *La Luna Grande* at the dock in Marina Hemingway, 9 miles west of Havana. He was there with his usual military entourage. Exiting his big Mercedes, he walked to the pier, accompanied by several uniformed soldiers walking a few steps behind.

The general had achieved a senior position in the government. His loyal service in the Cuban Revolution led him to be in Fidel's inner circle. The rank he held now was awarded more for his longevity than his ability. Like other aged generals, his Revolutionary Army status conferred privilege in Cuban society. The military ran the government's businesses and the old generals controlled the military. His waistline was clear evidence that his life was better than the average Cuban's.

General Diego reveled in his authority. Over the slightest error, he bullied the men and women detailed to be his personal guards. He was prone to slapping his hand to reinforce his orders. People took notice and steered clear of him, trying not to attract his attention. He was more feared than respected. Known as The General, it seemed only Captain Alvero had a special rapport with him, based on their long friendship, even if that friendship was not on equal terms.

As he approached the boat General Diego was delighted, anticipating that he would have a prize from Captain Alvero's clandestine expedition to Florida. Addressing the captain, Fernández and Costa, he said "So, gentlemen, please let me meet the notorious scum you have captured. I received your message from Key West that you had him in custody. Now, let me see the thief that stole the Crucifix of Friar Bartolomé de las Casas."

Agent Fernández climbed off the boat, followed by Detective Inspector Costa. Captain Alvero was still at the tower, avoiding any eye contact with his old friend, General Diego. Fernández said, "I'm afraid we lost him. He went…"

"What! ¡Mierda!" The general shouted, "I gave you two the assignment to capture the criminal and you failed! How incompetent you two must be!" Fernández timidly tried to explain but was interrupted repeatedly by the general's outbursts berating them for their failure.

Alvero then descended to the deck and looked at the general. He tried to explain, saying "It was my fault, General. I was going to slit the kid's throat on the way back, but the agents stopped me." Stumbling to tell the general what happened, the captain continued, "When I loosened my grip on him, he jumped off my… err, your…

boat, into the sea. We could not find him after searching for a long time. He must have drowned and is at the bottom of the ocean … with my grandson and my family that he did not save during the hurricane."

General Diego was still irate. However, he did not want to add more grief to his old friend, Alvero. He would focus his anger on the two agents sent to capture Matvey. He turned to them, "Why did you not have him secured? I expected you would either return with a prisoner or a body. This is not acceptable!"

After pausing to catch his breath, he continued. His anger was palpable. "It is not acceptable that a thief of our nation's treasures, even if it is a secret one, could escape punishment!"

The general was livid. No assurances that Matvey was likely dead assuaged his anger.

"Perhaps you three should take his place for punishment." He stomped away to his motorcade.

Fernández and Costa were without words. They silently looked at each other, each knowing they would face some consequence for not completing their mission.

THREE

Matvey floated in the warm water. The bright afternoon sun was warm on his face and he felt it burning. Washing salt water over his cheeks provided only temporary cooling relief, and then it stung his sunburned skin.

After floating for hours, occasionally having to kick his legs to maintain his buoyancy, he was nervous about the dangers of sharks or barracudas. Every bit of seaweed that touched his arm brought panic that he was being attacked. He was tiring as he tried to keep afloat. He thought, "Maybe a whale will come swallow me, like Jonah, and take me to shore." He fantasized he could ride on the back of a dolphin to safety.

He had no idea how long he had been in the water. It must have been all day because the sun was lowering in the sky. Soon it would set and he would be alone, in the dark. He wondered if he could survive the night. He knew swimming would be fruitless; it was 90 miles between the Florida Keys and Cuba. Even half that distance would be impossible to swim. After being in the water for so long his hands were puffy and wrinkled.

A wrack line of sargassum engulfed him, sending a surge of panic through his body. This large drifting floating mass of seaweed was thick. Pinfish nibbled at his bare ankles. He could see dorados, known as dolphin fish, darting about under the shadow of the floating wrack line. Matvey started to make his way through the floating algae, fighting to clear the path ahead of him to get to the other side.

As he swam, pushing the seaweed out of his way, he noticed trash trapped in the wrack. The litter had been drifting in the water until it had become ensnared by the mat of sargassum. He encountered a half-submerged beer can, plastic water bottles covered with barnacles, a broken Styrofoam ice chest, and a boat fender, all trapped in the floating mat. Matvey fought through the weeds, gathering refuse he could use for buoyancy. He kept the ice chest and boat fender, leaving the rest to float along with the seaweed. Clawing his way through the sargassum, he was again in the clear open water and the wrack line was drifting behind him.

Matvey used the rope attached to the boat fender to tie it to his wrist so it would not drift away. He broke the flimsy Styrofoam cooler into pieces that he stuffed under his shirt and in his pants legs. He struggled to arrange the foam in a way that would keep him upright in the water. Then, hanging on the boat bumper that he placed under his arms, he was comfortably floating, or as comfortable as anyone waterlogged in the middle of the ocean could be.

Each time he rose to the height of the sea swells, Matvey scanned the distance. When the sun dipped below the horizon he watched the afterglow of the sunset. The sky was reflecting

17

the final light, illuminated by the glow emanating from under the horizon. He knew that soon the twilight hour would give in to full darkness with only the moon and stars to illuminate the sea. Without solar radiation, the temperature dropped a few degrees and the wind picked up a little. A fresh breeze was rippling the surface of the water that had been calm with only swells.

The sun disappeared in the west. Matvey fought the urge to sleep, periodically dropping off, only to startle himself awake. Fortunately, the foam stuffed in his clothes and the fender were keeping him on the surface so he did not have to expend energy to tread water or float on his back.

His mind drifted over the past. Jumping from one topic to the next, he recalled past events before being distracted by the next thought. His mind raced through a thick fog of memories of his dead mother, their life as employees at the resort in Playa Girón, and how everything had changed.

He dozed and dreamed of his mother. She was calling him, "Matvey, ¡ven acá! Come here!" He awakened, startled, and, for an instant, was confused. He quickly regained awareness of his precarious situation.

He was unbearably sad thinking of his mother years after losing her when he was a teenager. She was too young to die, leaving him alone. Before he could cry, the thought popped into his head of Maria "la Gorda", the resort manager, helping him escape from the Girón Beach Club Resort and the police. Why did she do that for him? Why did Maria la Gorda come to his mind? He knew that "la Gorda" wasn't her real surname but he couldn't remember what it was. All of the resort staff called her "la Gorda", the fat lady, behind her back. Oh, how his mother had hated her.

He thought of the school teachers who would call him out for inattention to his studies. He remembered working at the resort, starting at a young age, alongside his mother. The staff had been nice to him, teaching him how to garden when he was little. Then, as a teenager, they taught him how to work in the kitchen, even how to cook. He loved getting a tip when he helped take the guests to their rooms. But most of all, he loved the dancing.

He thought of how he danced as a little boy with his mother and how graceful and beautiful she was when she danced for the resort's patrons. Then, after she died, and he was older, he danced with the lonely old ladies who came to stay at the resort. That thought made him check his pants pocket which reassured him that the bag of jewels he stole from those ladies was still there.

Matvey chided himself for thinking so erratically, saying out loud, "If you are going to survive, you need to be thinking clearly and stay focused." He reminded himself that he needed to keep an eye out for boats.

Then his mind wandered back to when he escaped Cuba on *La Luna* with Captain Alvero and his family. He recalled being caught in a hurricane and the terrifying journey in the turbulent seas, wind, and rain. He thought of the horrible crash on the Dry Tortugas reef and Captain Alvero's grandson and the kid's parents going overboard before the boat broke apart and flipped. He was thankful he hadn't been trapped under the boat.

His thoughts turned to Sunny, lovely Sunny, who found him washed ashore on the Loggerhead Key beach and took him to safety, feeding him, cleaning his scrapes from the reef, and helping him get to Key West. She even helped him find a job with the Bahamian caretaker, Henry Forbes, on her friend's large compound. Henry became a good friend to him and even took him back to the Dry Tortugas on a fishing trip. He recalled how he pestered Henry to go to Loggerhead Key on that trip. Henry didn't know that he intended to retrieve his box of jewelry and the historic cross of Friar Bartolomé that he buried in the sand near a monument. He remembered how angry he felt when he opened the box and discovered the gold cross was gone. But his jewels were still there.

Time seemed to pass slowly as Matvey hung on to the fender and drifted aimlessly in the dark. He was thankful he was still alive, while, at the same time, he wondered if he would die. Maybe this was his punishment for not saving Alvero's grandson when the old *La Luna* wrecked in the hurricane.

He was remembering how he washed ashore at Loggerhead Key, but Alvero's daughter and son-in-law, and their son, were lost at sea. He believed Captain Alvero also died when the small wooden boat sank, only to be shocked to see him again holding the tip of a knife at his throat, just before he jumped overboard, escaping certain death.

The memory of the young boy who had looked into his eyes with terror as he sank beneath the waves haunted Matvey. The boy's gaze burned into his soul, an image he could not forget. He tried to convince himself that he was not to blame and there was nothing he could have done to save the boy. He wondered, "Why did I survive, only to face this? Is this God's punishment?"

He felt bad about so many things. He regretted his tryst with the beautiful art professor, Evelyn. He was sorry about the misunderstanding when he mistakenly stole her cross and for hurting her when they struggled. With so much blood oozing from her forehead, he thought he had killed her. Until the two Cuban agents on the boat told him, he didn't know that Evelyn had survived. Although he stole a piece of jewelry from the lonely old ladies he seduced, he had not intended to steal the Crucifix of Friar Bartolomé from Evelyn.

He regretted being drunk during Sunny's crowded art show opening in Key West and accusing her of stealing the cross from the hiding place on Loggerhead. He had been so angry with her. And, then when he was forcefully removed from the building, Costa and Fernández were waiting outside for him. They captured him, shoved him into a car, and drove away, blindfolding and binding him. He remembered vividly the experience. It was astounding to learn that it was the captain who had taken the cross from its hiding place on the beach.

He wondered how long it had been since he was a captive on Captain Alvero's *La Luna Grande*. Was it yesterday or maybe it was today; he couldn't tell. He was angry that he had been captured in Key West, only to be in this present crisis.

Again, he scolded himself. "Matvey! Quit visiting the past and live in the present. Just look for a boat!"

He started to replace his resentment with searching the distant stretch of ocean for any sign that he was not alone in the ocean.

FOUR

Matvey floated in complete darkness. The moon was not yet rising. The sky was at its darkest, when, off in the far distance, he saw a faint glow of lights on both sides of his position. The illumination was so faint he wondered if it was real or just his imagination. He did not know if it could be the lights of Key West or Havana reflecting in the humid atmosphere, so he dismissed the vision as his imagination and stopped thinking about the dim blushes.

Unaware of time, Matvey watched the sky. He could see the Milky Way spread a faint mist of rainbow pastels across the heavens. He marveled at the millions of stars. With each meteor that streaked across the sky, he made a wish that he would be rescued. He could see what he speculated were satellites because they were brighter. He wished he was a passenger on the jet planes he saw flying overhead at high altitudes, following routes north and south. He wondered where the people in those planes were going, maybe to far-off destinations in South America or islands in the Caribbean. He wished they could see him and call someone to rescue him.

How beautiful was the night sky, but the expanse of darkness twinkling with myriad stars only added to his loneliness. He felt insignificant in the universe.

As a crescent moon rose, its light shined a pathway to the distant horizon. If only he could walk on the shimmering reflection he might reach land somewhere. Low in the water, clutching his boat fender, he was a prisoner of the ocean. As the moon climbed into the sky on its path transiting the heavens from east to west, the night spectacle of stars dimmed a little. Accustomed to the inky darkness, his eyes were fully dilated, allowing him to glimpse the endless waters surrounding him. Still, no boats were visible in the circumference of his vision, as he circled in the water continually scanning the horizon.

Matvey dozed off again. Slipping from his grip on the boat fender, he was awakened by the sea water covering his face. He swallowed a mouthful and choked on the salty water entering his airway. Coughing to clear his throat, he thought he heard music. Was it his imagination? He strained to listen. Yes, it was music!

Regaining his hold on the fender, he spun around to see where the sound might be coming from. It was a boat, a sailboat, with its sails ghostly illuminated from a light below. A red light was shining close to the water. He could not discern how far away the boat might be, but he started shouting and splashing in the water anyway.

Matvey heard a male voice command, "I want you to turn off that music. It's your bedtime!" Children's voices responded but, although he recognized the tone of protest, he could not make out what they were saying.

As the music quit, he yelled louder. He thrashed in the water creating a swirl of sparkling phosphorescence.

He could see no sign that the people on the sailboat saw him. Undeterred, Matvey increased his effort, bolstered by the adrenaline coursing through his veins. To attract their attention, he yelled in English, "Help! Help! I am here!" and in Spanish, "¡Oye! ¡Oye! ¡Aquí estoy! Hey! Hey! I am here!"

A child's voice rang out. "Dad, I see lights over there in the water! Maybe it's the dolphins playing in the water leaving their glowing neon tracks. Can we go see? Please?" Matvey continued to splash and yell. His splashing agitated the water, increasing the bioluminescence.

It seemed to take a while for the boat to change course. Eventually, it was coming toward him. Both red and green lights were visible just above the water. As the sailboat approached he could make out backlit silhouettes of two small figures standing at the bow pulpit. One was reflecting green and the other had a reddish cast. The two people appeared to be spirits in the glow of the boat's running lights.

Suddenly a bright spotlight on the foredeck came on and Matvey could clearly see children on the bow of the sailboat. Exuberant that he might be rescued, Matvey increased his activity and shouted with all his energy.

"Dad, I hear someone calling 'Help' where the water is glowing," one of the children shouted toward the back of the boat.

Matvey squinted when a bright spotlight hit his eyes. A man's voice shouted, "Hey Judy, come up on deck. I need your help. Kids get back here to the cockpit!"

A woman came up and gathered the children in the boat's cockpit as she said, "Mike, Linda, go below until I call you!"

Matvey saw the spotlight wander around. It was no longer pointed directly at him but was searching the surrounding waters.

Pat said, "Douse the main while I roll in the headsail furler. I'm starting the engine."

Now Matvey's shouting could not be heard over the noise of the engine, and the sailors' night vision had been lost when the bright spotlight was turned on. It became more difficult to locate anyone in the water. Matvey saw the boat turn, but it was turning away!

"No! No! No!" Matvey yelled, "Come back, I am here!! ¡Aqui! ¡Oye! ¡Aqui estoy!"

The sailboat was getting farther away as it turned in circles searching for him. The futility and frustration of calling out to them was exasperating. Matvey could only hope they would return and find him. Slowly the boat circled back closer to his position. The kids were back on deck and all eyes were searching the dark water. When the deck light was turned off and the engine stopped, the boat was quiet and drifting.

Matvey started to yell again while splashing the water. He heard the sound of a girl shrieking, "Over there – I see someone!" This gave Matvey hope.

The bright spotlight came on again and lit him up. The light hurt his eyes. But he kept flailing his arms over his head, in spite of the boat fender tied to one arm hampering his motion. The light stayed on him as the engine started sputtering again, and the boat headed right for him.

Piloting the boat to Matvey's position took a few minutes. He continued a gentle sweep of his free arm, bathed in the beam of the spotlight. That light was his beacon of salvation.

Soon he was alongside the hull of the boat. The engine was still running, and Matvey feared he would be cut by the propeller.

He shouted, "Please don't run over me! Please save me from the sea!" He didn't realize how hoarse he had become from yelling for help. He could not believe that he was being rescued.

The man and woman on the sailboat threw him a line that was tied to the boat as they shouted to him over the engine noise. "Can you climb a ladder to get on board?" Matvey worked his way along the line to the boat's stern. He thought certainly he could get on the boat, until he tried. His legs were like noodles. The surge of energy he had while yelling and thrashing faded quickly.

Seeing this, the man said, "Judy, I'll heave-to to make it easier to get him on board. Make a loop he can get around himself and we will hoist him up using the topping lift line."

Once Matvey was holding onto the boat's swim platform, the couple made sure the boat was stable. Matvey was still afraid he might be shredded by the propeller, even though the boat's engine was not in gear. They let out the headsail a little and then hove to with the rudder in a fixed position to keep the boat into the wind and the deeply-reefed headsail backed to windward. The boat was then drifting sideways being moved forward by the current and pushed sideways by a gentle breeze. The two children were wide-eyed watching this amazing rescue at sea.

Judy said, "OK Pat, give me a minute." Then, to Matvey, she continued, "Mister, can you put a loop around under your arms when I throw this rope to you?" Matvey nodded. He had a firm grip on the swim ladder.

Now that he was hanging onto the boat, she could safely retrieve the line she had thrown him and tie a loop in it. As Matvey put the loop over his head and under his arms, she attached her end of the line to the mainsail boom. The line that holds up the end of the boom when the mainsail is not up, the topping lift, would be used to get him on board. Matvey untied the boat fender from his wrist and put it on the swim platform.

After hooking the topping lift shackle to the line around Matvey, Pat and Judy put the other end of the topping lift line on a winch and cranked on it to raise the end of the boom. As the boom went up, the line under Matvey's arms became taut and their exhausted swimmer was raised up from the ocean and onto the boat. Once on board, Matvey tried to stand but immediately crumpled to the deck, exhausted.

Judy brought a gallon jug of fresh water and doled out a little at a time. Matvey was thirsty and gulped down each cupful. Pat helped Matvey off the deck onto a cushion on the cockpit seat. He leaned back creating a bizarre disfigured shape and revealing that his soaked garments were stuffed with foam.

All he could mumble, over and over, was "Thank you for rescuing me. Thank you. ¡Gracias! Thank you so much. You save my life!"

About a half hour passed before Matvey was finally a little more lucid. Of course, Pat and Judy were curious about his circumstances, how he got into the water, and where he came from. Before they could ask, the children began an interrogation. Speaking at once, they asked, "What is your name? How did you get here? Where are you from? How long were you in the ocean? Were you scared? Did you see any sharks?"

Matvey was slow to respond to their rapid-fire inquiries. He was tired and still a little confused. It was difficult for him to think in English to answer all of their questions. He wanted to answer their questions with the truth, but he also wanted to be careful not to reveal too much truth.

"I am sorry. My English is not so good. My name is Matvey Valdez Descon. I am from Cuba. I was on a boat but fell off. I am tired now. May I have more water, por favor?"

Judy asked, "Was there anybody else in the water with you? Should we be looking for another person?"

Matvey shook his head no. Since this was not definitive enough for Judy she asked again until Matvey replied. "No one. I am the only one who went over."

Knowing that there was nobody else that needed rescuing, Pat and Judy instructed Mike and Linda to go below and get in bed.

"That's enough excitement for you two for tonight."

The kids were pumped up from the intensity of rescuing someone and learning that he came all the way from Cuba. It took several admonitions from Judy for them to quiet down and finally head to their bunks.

Matvey became aware of the discomfort from the foam stuffed in his clothes and began extracting the pieces from his shirt and pants. Judy collected it and stowed it. She didn't want all that flotation foam to end up back in the ocean as more plastic garbage.

Matvey sipped the water, closed his eyes and soon was asleep, leaning on the cabin bulkhead.

Pat decided, "Let's let him sleep. He can use the tarp for a blanket. We'll get him dried off and a change of clothes when he wakes up. We should raise the sails and get back underway. He seems OK for now." Judy agreed and the two raised the mainsail and returned to their course.

Judy suggested they both should stand watch together tonight instead of taking shifts. "We don't know much about this refugee. Let's be careful."

Through the night, Pat and Judy talked quietly about their rescue of Matvey. Their initial questions had not been answered and, as they sailed through the night, they had so many more. They watched the young man, slumped in the cockpit corner against the bulkhead in a deep sleep, wrapped in a tarp. They would have to wait until morning to get answers and to clean up this new passenger on their boat. For now, they would continue their plans to sail to Bimini to clear immigration and customs. If their rescuee was not well, they would divert to Florida or call the Coast Guard. All they could do now was wait until morning to see how he was faring.

FIVE

Dawn's early light painted the eastern sky in a subdued palette. Pink and violet smeared on a yellow canvas preceded the sunrise. As the morning sky turned brighter with the sunrise, Matvey stirred.

Judy had coffee ready. Matvey was still soaked and shivering in the early morning breeze. He was very happy to have hot coffee, even if it was Americano and not espresso or café con leche.

Judy introduced herself saying, "My name is Judy. Um ... mi nombre es Judy. And this is my husband Pat. Él es mi esposo Pat. We live aboard with our two children, dos hijos, Michael and Linda. We were on our way to The Bahamas when Linda heard you calling."

As the kids woke and came into the cockpit, Judy brought out some muffins. Seas were still calm with a gentle breeze on the aft quarter. They continued their slow broad reach, boosted by the Gulf Stream's current.

Matvey gobbled up the muffins and had an unquenchable thirst. Pat wondered if he would drink up all their freshwater supply before they reached Bimini in The Bahamas.

Matvey was recuperating and beginning to feel like himself. He had no injuries from his time in the ocean, but he was sunburned and felt itchy from dried salt on his skin. He was happy to be alive. At every chance he humbly expressed his gratitude to his rescuers. In the light of day, he felt his prospects were looking up.

Judy pulled out a set of Pat's clothes for Matvey to wear. He could finally get out of his wet shirt and trousers. Judy directed the kids to go below while Matvey bathed on the foredeck. She and Pat diverted their attention from watching him use a bucket of seawater and saltwater soap to wash. Even trying to be respectful of his privacy, Judy glimpsed the tall, well-toned, youthful body naked on the foredeck. He was quite a physical specimen. With wavy blonde hair and jewel-like emerald green eyes, his appearance was so unlike the Cubans she had met in Key West.

In dry clothes that mostly fit, Matvey felt rejuvenated and energetic. He responded to the multiple questions that they all had for him. He told a story that wasn't quite the truth, but he thought it might be believable to the American sailors.

"My name is Matvey Valdez Descon," not remembering that he had already told them his name the night before. Struggling to think of the English words, he continued slowly, "I am from Cuba. I was on a large boat, crowded with Cubans trying to escape horrible conditions in Cuba to get to the Estados Unidos. The weather got a little rough and the traffickers who were taking us did not seem to care that we were overloaded. It was at night and I was… uh," he paused trying to think of a polite way to say "pissing." Continuing, he said, "Making water over the side of the boat when I fell off. I could not believe that the boat kept going. The Captain already had my money, so he didn't care if I was gone and he had one less human cargo to deliver to some islands near Key West."

"Wow. That's heartless!" exclaimed Pat. "How long were you in the water?"

Judy was able to speak and understand a little Spanish, so she conversed with Matvey in the language that was easier for him. Occasionally she would stop and update Pat on what they were discussing.

"I don't know, but at least all day and into the night when you found me. I was lucky to find the thing to float on in the sea plants. I was so afraid of sharks."

Matvey grabbed his wet clothes from Judy, who was about to hang them up on the lifelines to dry. He turned away and retrieved something out of the pocket, stuffing it into his new dry britches.

"Thank you, but I do not want to be more trouble to you. I can hang my pants and shirt to dry." Judy recognized he had something he did not want her to see.

Pat and Judy respected his privacy, but they still needed to decide what they should do. Speaking to Matvey, Judy said, "We plan to go to The Bahamas. Will you be OK to get off there? Will they return you to Cuba? We prefer not to divert to Florida."

"I don't know. I paid the trafficker to get me to the U.S. and make the arrangements to get asylum. In The Bahamas, I don't know what is the procedure. I think they have diplomatic relations with Cuba and might send me back. If they do, I will be in big trouble."

"Well, Matvey, we don't want to get in trouble ourselves. Surely there is some exception for someone rescued at sea."

"I don't have a passport or any of my things. They are on the trafficker's boat. I have no identification. Maybe you can let me off somewhere and I will find my way on my own. You should not be in trouble for your kindness."

Pat said, "Let's just decide what to do when we get to The Bahamas. We will have Internet sometime before we check in at a port. We can try to look up the rules. For now, let's just be thankful that you are alive."

"OK, I can wait. I want to help you sail the boat or do any jobs you have for me."

"When you are back to full speed, you can help. For now, just rest and get your strength back. You have been through a lot."

Matvey spent the day resting and talking to the children on the foredeck. He was giving spontaneous Spanish lessons to the children, naming things in Spanish and asking Mike and Linda to repeat the words. He quizzed them frequently to be sure they were learning.

Both children were engaged with this new passenger and excited to be learning something from the mysterious castaway they had rescued. Matvey was happy to be focused on teaching Spanish rather than having to discuss his story about falling overboard.

Pat and Judy were back in the cockpit talking quietly about how to handle having an unknown guest on board. Looking up to the foredeck, Judy observed, "He seems to be good with the children."

Pat replied, "Yes, but we still don't know anything about him. I think we should be careful. Something about his story doesn't quite add up. The weather has been clear, so the rough seas throwing him overboard ...."

Judy interrupted, "Pat, maybe he got his timeframe mixed up. And, rough weather is, well, relative."

Pat shrugged. "Maybe you're right. But, I think we still need to be careful. He's young and strong. On the positive side, he can stand watch with me at night. Then I can keep an eye on him.

You can take the helm during the day. If he's tired from staying up, maybe he will sleep during the day. Just a thought."

Judy smiled. "You're probably right. I'll start steering now and you get some rest. Everything is fine at the moment. I'll ring our emergency bell if I need you."

Later, at dinner, Matvey was full of questions for his hosts. If he was asking questions about them, he was off the hook on having to explain more about his circumstances.

"Where were you coming from when you picked me up out of the sea?"

Judy started, "We left Key West earlier yesterday. We had been stuck there for months. After a hurricane hit the Keys last year we had some damage and all of the boatyards were backed up with recovery and repairs. So many boats were sunk or washed up into the mangroves."

Mike interrupted. "Before we got to the Keys we were at a neat island with a fort and one with a lighthouse. There was a nice lady there who told us about sea turtles."

Linda corrected her little brother. "We were in the Dry Tortugas at Fort Jefferson. Then we went to Loggerhead Key and met a lady who was an artist. Her name was Sunny and she lived in a house next to the lighthouse." From the neck of her tee shirt, she pulled out a necklace with a seashell strung on the end. "She gave me this to remember her."

Mike added, "She gave me one, too!"

Pat continued with their story. "We got out of those islands, they are about 70 miles west of Key West, just in time to find a safe place to ride out the hurricane. That hurricane went right over the Tortugas. We often wonder if Sunny and the rangers in the fort made it through the storm okay."

Matvey wanted to admit that he knew Sunny and she was okay, but that would undermine the story he had already shared. He had learned long ago that, in some situations, it was best not to say anything, so he held his tongue and feigned astonishment. Matvey closed his eyes, picturing Sunny. He recalled again how she had saved him when he washed up on the shore of Loggerhead Key after the terrible hurricane. She had been an angel and, in the end, he treated her so terribly by accusing her of theft. Instead of mentioning Sunny, he said to the family, "Was that scary for you? Were you on this boat during the hurricane?"

Pat said, "No. We took refuge ashore in Key West in a small building, on the second floor. The ground floor flooded. Our boat was anchored and tied to a mooring ball."

"Mooring ball? I don't know what is that?"

Judy said, "It's a big anchor of concrete on the sea floor that has a chain and a float attached to it. The float at the surface is where you tie your boat line. It's a big round ball. Most times it is more secure than an anchor because it's bigger and heavier than an anchor."

Pat interrupted, "We put out our anchor, too, just in case and to help with the strain of the wind and waves pushing the boat. We don't know exactly what happened but after the storm when we got back to the boat, we found the side was cracked around the chainplates."

"Chainplates? I do not understand all of the names for things on a boat."

Pat jumped to his feet, "Let me show you. This is our home, a 35-foot sloop. We named her *Sunshine* because we want to sail the *sunshine*! A sloop is a boat with a single mast and sail, and one sail on the front of the boat called a jib. Boats with different configurations of sails are called different names."

Matvey put up a hand to indicate stop. "Wait, wait! This is too fast! There are too many, err, things I do not understand."

Pat walked to the beam deck and pointed to the metal bars protruding up through the deck. Trying to speak slowly and explain more clearly, Pat continued, "Wires are attached to these to keep the mast up. These are called chainplates." He paused so Matvey could think about these new concepts. "The wires are called shrouds and stays. The one in the front is a forestay. The one in the back is a backstay."

Learning about the sailboat, with new names in English, was overwhelming for Matvey. He said, "These boat names are hard! But, I will try to remember." He repeated as he pointed to each, "Backstay, forestay, shrouds. chainplates. Sí?"

Pat joked, "No, the sea is over the side," pointing to the water.

There was an inquisitive look on Matvey's face while he processed the joke. "Oh yes, *sí* is yes, and *the sea* is wet!"

They both chuckled and returned to the cockpit. Matvey helped Judy and the kids clear the table. He insisted on doing the dishes. Judy had to caution him about using too much of their limited supply of fresh water.

Matvey said, "I have so much to learn about the boat and still much to learn about improving my English."

Pat and Judy were feeling a little more comfortable because of Matvey's affable good nature. Maybe he would be OK. Their anxiety about pirates taking boats had been fueled by horror stories in cruising magazines. They would still be cautious, but this handsome young man seemed harmless enough and a bit naive.

After dinner, Pat informed Matvey about how things would go at night. The two of them would stand watch together. Matvey's job was looking for ships transiting the Gulf Stream while *Sunshine* was on her way northward toward Bimini.

Pat said, "In light of your immigration problem, we think we will bypass checking in with Bahamas immigration at Bimini and go to Riding Rocks instead." Pointing to the chart, he continued, "It's a little south of Bimini. We can stop to rest there. Then we will head over to Andros and maybe anchor overnight at Cross Cays. Then we could sail on to Morgan's Bluff. We might check in with immigration there or go straight to Nassau on New Providence. It's all up in the air. That's how cruising is on a sailboat." He smiled, then said, "As long as we are at sea and don't go to a port, we don't have to check in and provide passports. So unless we are boarded by The Bahamas Defense Force you should be OK."

As darkness overtook the ocean, Judy and the kids retreated to the cabin. Before heading down, Mike embraced Matvey in a warm hug. After spending just a little time together, the children had bonded with this new passenger.

Pat went through the night routine again, showing Matvey the course they would steer through the night to reach Riding Rocks the next afternoon. Pat and Matvey donned windbreakers and personal flotation devices. Pat explained, "It's a rule aboard that, when sailing at night, you must wear your PFD and the harness that is attached to the PFD must be secured to the boat. We don't want anyone going overboard, but if they do, they'll be attached to the boat, not lost at sea."

With a calm breeze, the Gulf Stream was not rough. They were making good time in the current. The evening went smoothly. Matvey took the wheel while being mentored by Pat about how to follow a course and keep the sails full. He seemed to have a natural knack for sailing, at least in calm conditions.

SIX

Arriving midday at Riding Rocks, Judy took the helm and started the engine as Pat brought in the sails and stood on the bow. He wanted to watch for the shallow reefs bordering the deep water of the Florida Straits. The chart showed that the depth quickly declines from over a thousand feet to shallow rocky ledges that could ground a boat. In the past many unsuspecting Spanish galleons wrecked on these reefs, not anticipating such a drastic change in depth. With modern navigation electronics, it was easier to know a boat's position relative to the reef.

But, even with the GPS plotter showing the depth and course, experience had taught Pat and Judy that eyeball navigation is essential. When he saw the darker shadows of reefs, Pat motioned to Judy to steer clear of the potential hazards and into clear green water that indicated a sandy bottom. When the depth sounder revealed they were in about 12 feet of water and Pat sighted they were in the lee of a low-lying rocky island shore, he used hand signals to communicate with Judy. She slowed the boat and turned into the wind, gliding to a stop before reversing the engine to stop the forward motion of the boat. Pat let out their anchor rode, watching through crystal clear water as the anchor hit the bottom. Then Pat motioned a backward movement and Judy put the motor in reverse to set the hook. The boat swung hard and stopped. The anchor was set.

Making landfall in the afternoon sun was easy. Pat could see the bottom. At night or under overcast skies, the operation would have been far more stressful. With a confident set of the anchor, they could relax and be able to sleep through the night.

Pat took a moment to show Matvey where they were on the navigation plotter.

"This is where we are now. It is named Riding Rocks." Pat expanded the view on the plotter and continued, "This is about where we picked you from the ocean, nearly 40 miles back."

Matvey asked, "What is that in kilometers?"

Pat calculated the distance. "Well, maybe about 65," he said hesitantly. "I don't know exactly."

Then, Pat showed him the locations where they might be heading next. "This is Bimini. This is Andros. We may even make it to Nassau. And, this is Miami, in Florida." Kidding Matvey, Pat said, "I hear that all Cubans have a cousin there."

Mike and Linda were patient while *Sunshine* was being anchored. As soon as the anchor was down they started pestering, "Can we go ashore? Let's explore the island. Maybe we will find buried pirate treasure!"

Pat acquiesced to their pleading and launched the dinghy from its davits. "We are not supposed to go ashore until we clear immigration. But, there's nobody around and this is just a deserted rock, so we can chance it for a little while."

The kids shouted excitedly, "C'mon Matvey, let's go to the island and find some treasure!"

Matvey was reminded of his treasure and fondled the bag of jewels he had surreptitiously slipped out of his wet pants and into the pocket of the pants Pat loaned him.

As the kids and Matvey were getting into the dinghy, Pat asked, "Judy, would you mind staying on the boat to make sure we don't drift?"

Judy nodded as she said, "Some alone time would actually be nice. I might even be able to read a chapter or two!"

Pat found a soft sand beach to land the dinghy and the kids took off treasure hunting. Amid the piles of seaweed, Mike and Linda's beach combing was unproductive. Plastic trash and boat debris littered the wrack line. Flotsam in the sea became garbage on the shore, spoiling the pristine rocky island. Because of their activity on the beach, a few gulls and shorebirds loafing on the island took flight. After an hour of exploring, it was time to get back to the boat. Mike and Linda were instructed to leave their beach combing prizes behind for someone else to find.

Judy had dinner prepared by the time they returned. Over the meal, Matvey returned to his questions.

"Have you always lived on this boat? Where are you from - the Estados Unidos? Where are you going? Is The Bahamas the end of your voyage?"

Matvey's endless curiosity kept the family busy answering his many questions. The conversation was interesting to him and, more importantly, kept his story from being discussed.

Finally, Pat said, "Enough about us. How about telling us more about you and your life in Cuba."

Matvey was okay with revealing this part of his story. He could safely tell about his life growing up at the Caribbean resort on Cuba's southern shore. He revealed his mother was a professional dancer and that he sometimes danced with her during her shows for the tourists. He told them how the workers at the resort were kind to him and taught him many skills.

Matvey shared how life in Cuba was both wonderful and terrible at the same time. "The country is beautiful and our people are happy. The government is well-meaning but crazy. Some rules are stupid and punishment is harsh."

The family was intrigued to learn about Cuba from a Cuban rather than from the spin of the official U.S. government position and political rhetoric.

Matvey continued, "In Cuba, there is music and dancing. We have a long tradition of stories. People get by difficult shortages by being … how you say?…. innovator…err, ingenious?"

Judy suggested, "Do you mean innovative? Is that the word?"

"Yes," he agreed, smiling. "¡Sí! The yes one, not the wet one! Innovative. People survive with what they have or the opportunities they can make. It helps that there is a big underground market where you can trade for things. Our Cuban peso is worthless!"

"I miss Cuba, but I need to start a new life. I see on the Internet…" He paused to explain, "We got the Internet a few years ago in Cuba. Now we see that the rest of the world is different and all Americans are rich. I want to work hard and become rich, too!"

Pat and Linda laughed. "You are so wrong! Not all Americans are rich. Most struggle to get by. A few people have all the money and want the rest of us to remain poor."

Matvey was puzzled to hear this from people who were on their own boat and able to sail as a lifestyle. He accepted that their reply must be true, even if it did not fit his understanding of the U.S. and his experience in Key West.

Pat and Judy rigged an outside shelter in the cockpit where Matvey could sleep. He could stand watch, periodically checking on their position to make sure the anchor did not pull out and set them adrift. It was a plausible explanation for not inviting him into the cabin. At least not yet, not until he had their full trust and confidence. Besides, in decent weather, the family would often sleep on deck in the cool breeze.

After a ration of rum as a nightcap for the adults, the family retired. Matvey stayed awake watching the stars. It was different and a pleasure to view the celestial display from the safety of a boat rather than his waterlogged isolation, bobbing in the ocean. He went to sleep thankful and hopeful this second chance would turn out well for him.

SEVEN

Pat and Judy abandoned plans to check in at Bimini. Being remote and having fewer visitors, Andros appeared to be a better, more suitable option for Matvey. They might be able to avoid the immigration process on Andros, putting it off for as long as possible.

As they approached Morgan's Bluff, everyone was pleased to see the signs of human habitation ashore. They had been on the boat for three nights without any sight of other people. They could see they were at a destination where they might be able to get some supplies. Having to feed an additional person, a hungry young man, had not been planned and they needed water and a few staples.

Pat went ashore alone in the dinghy with two jerry cans for water and a wish list for shopping. He was careful to avoid checking in with immigration, which they now hoped to do in Nassau. They knew it was not legal to come ashore without checking in but they did not want to be caught with an undocumented passenger. It would only cause problems for them and Matvey. If Pat was stopped by an immigration official, he would then go through the process as if it had been planned all along, hoping for the best outcome for Matvey.

As is the practice when arriving in a new country, Judy raised the Bahamas quarantine flag and courtesy burgee on the spreader halyard to show they were a visiting yacht. Of course, most often any sailing yacht would be visiting because the boats Bahamians used were not like Pat and Judy's auxiliary cruiser. They were skiffs, working boats, or Bahamas sloops used for competitive racing. With their distinctive rigging and large sails, Bahamas sloops were a sight to see.

Pat returned with water jugs filled and a boat bag filled with groceries. As he pulled up he said, "They didn't have much in the little store, but I got a few things. And, I got us all a treat!"

As he handed the bag to Judy, she was delighted to see a half gallon of ice cream. "Quick, kids, get cups and spoons. This is going to melt soon, so we better have our dessert for lunch!"

They all sat in the cockpit enjoying their ice cream treat, which was more like a milkshake than ice cream. What a wonderful and unexpected surprise. Ice cream is not something one finds on many cruising sailboats. Maybe big luxury yachts would have a freezer, but what is on most sailboats, like theirs, is usually just a refrigerator.

Matvey said, "In Cuba, we call this helado. It has been a long time since I had helado."

"I didn't see an immigration official to check in with. It seems they were occupied down south and the locals said tomorrow is a holiday. They thought we could just check in in Nassau." That meant that *Sunshine* could legally fly a yellow quarantine flag while they continued to round the eastern shore of Andros.

Judy had researched Andros when planning their Bahamas trip while they were stuck in Key West waiting for repairs to their boat. In all the cruising guides to the Bahamas, the group of islands that are collectively called Andros was touted to be the largest land mass in the entire Bahamas archipelago. There were several places they wanted to check out before they headed to Nassau.

She relayed to her family and Matvey, "The national park on Andros is acclaimed for the number of blue holes within its 40,000 acres of pinelands and coppice. One blue hole I read about is Captain Bill's Blue Hole. It's on my wish list for places to go in The Bahamas."

Since it was a national holiday, they decided not to wait for Immigration and Customs in Morgan's Bluff. While they were technically not cleared in, Pat and Judy thought it was worth the risk to go ashore to the national park. They wanted to take the kids swimming in fresh water. It would be a treat for everyone after having to ration their onboard water supplies for the past week. Mike and Linda were excited at the prospect of swimming in the amazing "bottomless pit" of a blue hole.

Plugging their destination into their GPS plotter, they headed south from Morgan's Bluff to the cut in the barrier reef at Fresh Creek on the eastern side of Andros. While underway Judy said to Mike and Linda, "Kids, before we go swimming in a blue hole, I want to give you a little geology lesson." She read, or rather paraphrased, from the guide book. "A blue hole is a circular pool with high limestone walls. Some are hundreds of feet deep. Some have been explored by divers who have discovered a labyrinth of caves beneath the water's surface. Divers have even found fossils in blue holes, on ledges in the walls or on the bottom."

Matvey was interested and listening, too.

Linda was puzzled. "What is a lab-a-rinth?"

Judy continued, "Over thousands of years, the limestone that makes up this island dissolved, creating the holes and caves. Some of the holes are deep enough to allow sea water to seep in from below. When it rains, the fresh water pools in the big holes. And because fresh water is lighter than sea water, blue holes have a freshwater surface and salt water at the bottom. There are even blue holes out in the waters surrounding some of the Bahamas islands, but they are called 'ocean holes'. A labyrinth, in this case, is rocks full of holes, like Swiss cheese."

After anchoring off Andros Town settlement, they dinghied to shore to visit Captain Bill's Blue Hole to go swimming. They hitched a ride in an open pickup truck. The driver was very friendly and even offered to pick them up in a couple of hours on his way back from running errands in Morgan's Bluff on the north end of the island.

When they got to the Blue Hole, they found a small pavilion and an open platform for high diving. Seeing the height, both Mike and Linda quickly backed away from the edge. Their enthusiasm was tempered by self-preservation. It appeared to be a long way down to the water.

Matvey and the family walked the circumference trail around the pond. There were few places to get in or out of the water because of the steep rock walls. The platform pavilion would be the best place to enter and exit.

They descended the stairs to the water's edge and swam in the cool and clear water. Refreshing fresh water bathed their sun and salt-soaked skin. After getting acclimated to the blue hole, the kids were a little more adventurous and decided they would jump into the water from the high platform.

Pat and Judy helped them to the edge of the deck. Matvey was in the water. Linda had the bravado to go first. "Wheee!" She took a flying leap off the platform and landed butt-first in the pond. She got out and climbed back up to the deck. Taunting her little brother, she said, "See a girl can do it! Are you a chicken?"

Mike snapped back, "No! I am not a chicken. I am an osprey diving to catch a fish."

With that, Mike leaped to the water, landing with a belly flop that resonated an echo off the rock walls. Initially, it seemed funny. Then there was panic. The indelicate landing knocked Mike's breath away, and he was sinking into the depths of the blue hole. He was momentarily stunned and choked on water that he autonomically inhaled.

Matvey saw the boy hit the water and then not surface. He quickly swam to the site of the splash and dove underwater. Ten feet down, Mike was disoriented and sinking fast. Matvey grabbed Mike's arm and kicked hard to the surface. Pat and Judy slid down the rocky path to the water's edge. Matvey had lifesaving training at the resort in Girón, so he immediately started clearing Mike's airway and expelling the water. Mike coughed up a mouthful and his eyes opened wide.

"What happened?" He coughed.

Judy sobbed, "Oh, Michael! We thought we lost you! You were sinking but Matvey saved you." She hugged her sopping-wet little boy tightly.

Sitting back a few feet from the joyous family, Matvey felt redeemed from his failure to act when Alvero's grandson was lost overboard. He realized that this near tragedy was an opportunity for him to choose to do the right thing. This time he had no box full of treasures to secure. Although his actions today did not resurrect the boy he did not save, he felt good that he had saved Mike.

Pat was shaken that he had almost lost his son and immensely thankful that Matvey was there. The hole was so deep that Mike might have never made his way back to the surface. To cover his raw feelings of concern and relief, he said, "That's enough swimming. Let's go back to the boat."

Mike resented the constant smothering attention from the rest of the family as they walked all the way back to the boat. He was fine. As an independent lad, his precarious brush with drowning made no impression on him. It was clear that his parents were moved and did not know how to express their gratitude to Matvey.

That night after dinner the couple stayed up late sharing rum with Matvey in the cockpit. They were anchored offshore and not near the dock at Fresh Creek. Fortunately, the seas and wind were dead calm or this anchorage would have been untenable.

"Matvey, I don't know how to thank you for saving Mike today at the blue hole. Words and hugs are not enough. What can we do for you?"

Judy was tearful. "We might have lost him. It happened so fast. If you had not been there…"

Matvey said "No problem. I am happy I was there. Maybe it is my chance to do something for you. You save me from the sea. I help to save tu hijo, your son, from the blue hole."

Pat said, "Tomorrow we will leave with the sunrise and sail to Nassau where we'll check in since we missed the immigration folks here."

Matvey was sullen and silent.

Judy asked, "Is something the matter?"

"Yes." Matvey was more forthcoming about his situation. He continued with a plausible story about why he couldn't approach Bahamas immigration. "Like I said, I do not have a passport. I did not tell you the whole story before. I was afraid you would put me back in the sea. The reason I was on the boat to escape Cuba was because the government wanted to arrest me for political crimes. The traffickers have my passport."

"Can't you apply for asylum?" Pat commented.

Matvey said, "In the U.S. maybe, but Cuba and the Bahamas have agreements for returning prisoners. I heard that Cubans caught trying to get to here are sent back and jailed. Prisons in Cuba are hard places."

Pat said, "I think prisons anywhere are hard."

"My only hope is to hide in the Bahamas until I can find some way to get to the U.S. I am sorry I didn't tell you that I am a fugitive from the Cuban government, not just a person seeking a better life – a refugee. I was afraid you would think I am a bad person and not save me. I do not want to cause you trouble. You have been so kind."

Pat was a little peeved. If they had known the full story earlier, they would have diverted to Florida. He realized Matvey being aboard as some kind of political criminal could have been very bad if they had been caught by Bahamas immigration at the Blue Hole. He couldn't be too angry though because Matvey just saved his son.

Pat poured another rum and looked at his iPad to plot a course, while he said, "I've got to think about this." Turning to Judy he suggested, "Look up on the cruisers forum for places to anchor before checking in with immigration on New Providence."

Pat plotted a route from Fresh Creek to New Providence. It was not too far, only 20 nautical miles across the Tongue of the Ocean. He could see on his GPS plotter that this body of water is very deep, surrounded by islands and reefs. Andros is on the west and shallow waters are on the eastern side, off the Exumas. A shallow and rocky rim borders the south.

Judy spoke up, "There's a place on the southwest of New Providence called Clifton Bay. It's between a park, some kind of historical site, and Lyford Cay, an upscale private enclave. A large bay there is noted as an anchorage to wait in before going into Nassau Harbor, which is to the north and east. Reviews are good."

"Well, how about we go there to anchor before going around to clear at Nassau Harbor? We can take Matvey to shore at the park after dark. Then, Matvey, it will be up to you to blend into the populace. What do you think?"

"I think that will be good. I can find my way around. Maybe there are tourists, and I can find a friend. Most importantly, you will not be caught trafficking me. I do not want you to get in trouble."

Pat said, "Fine, it's a plan. We will sail off when the sun comes up and we can find our way out through the reef. We will leave before the Andros Immigration Office reopens in the morning."

Sailing over to New Providence was leisurely. Pat let Matvey take the helm while he continued coaching him on steering and how to trim the sails. They were enjoying sailing in light air, tacking often to head east in easterly winds. The twenty-mile run took most of the day, from morning to early afternoon.

Ten boats were anchored in the Clifton Bay. More kept joining them throughout the afternoon. Tenders were going to shore to enjoy Jaws Beach. Judy's cruising guide indicated that this was one of the Bahamas' best beaches, certainly the best on the island of

New Providence. The guide noted that the beach and adjacent forest had been preserved in a national park for the public to enjoy. Judy reset the yellow quarantine flag indicating they had not cleared immigration and customs. Many of the boats in the harbor were flying their quarantine flag so *Sunshine* did not stand out.

There was time for launching the dinghy and taking the kids to nearby Goulding Cay for a little beach combing. Matvey enjoyed walking along the shore with Mike and Linda. They showed him their prize finds for him to admire. When they returned to the boat, Pat tied the dinghy to the stern with a long painter.

The children were unaware Matvey would be leaving them soon. Pat and Judy thought it best that they not know he would be departing. If they did not have a secret to keep, it would be safer for Matvey. The less they knew the better.

After dinner, Pat and Judy put the kids to bed. When the children were sound asleep, Pat brought the dinghy to the swim platform. Judy prepared a knapsack with a change of clothes, a bottle of water, a couple of energy bars, and a tarp he could use as a tent. Pat gave him a light windbreaker with a hood. Before leaving the boat, Matvey hugged Judy warmly and thanked her for helping him. Both had tears in their eyes.

When Matvey and Pat reached shore it was very dark. The park was closed so Matvey would have the beach to himself. Pat shook his hand and gave him $120 in U.S. dollars. It was a heartfelt farewell even if quick and unsentimental. As Pat was getting the dinghy ready to shove off the shore, Matvey hugged Pat tightly, saying, "Gracias, mi amigo! You save my life. I cannot thank you enough!"

Returning to *Sunshine*, Pat looked back to where he left Matvey on the beach. His head was spinning as he thought, that, over just three days, they had rescued the overboard Cuban, and come to care for him. Matvey had repaid the favor by saving his son's life. Now, this chance meeting was ending, and Matvey faced an uncertain future.

EIGHT

In the moonlight, Matvey wandered from the beach into the coppice forest, finding many gravel trails. He occasionally saw signs with an arrow pointing to one place or another. But, none of it made any sense to him. He knew from Judy's explanation that he was in a park, but he had no idea where he was in the park or on the island for that matter. He had briefly seen the chart on the boat's GPS plotter. However, on the nautical chart, there wasn't much detail about the land. He sensed that Nassau was some distance away, but he had no idea how far or even in what direction to head. He wondered if the city was close enough that he could walk there.

One of the trails led him to a ruin of an old colonial plantation dwelling located fairly close to the beach. He reasoned this would be a good shelter for the night. He planned to act like a park visitor when the sun came up. He would try to meet someone to learn more about where he was and then devise a plan to get to Nassau.

He continued to explore his surroundings by the light of the moon. He walked on one trail that led up to a paved road. No cars were traveling the road at night. He wondered if the road went to Nassau and whether it would be busy enough in the daytime that he could hitch a ride with someone, like he used to do in Cuba.

He was confused by all of the different paths when he tried to find his way back to the little stone ruin where he planned to spend the night. He didn't want to be at the roadside in case the police came by, so he retraced the route he thought he had walked.

Turning the corner, he saw a golf cart driving toward him. Matvey quickly retreated to the brush to let two guys on the golf cart pass. As they moved by, he could see they were security guards patrolling the park. It was lucky he had noticed them before they noticed him. He needed to find a better place than the little stone house to hide for the rest of the night. He heard them chatter about going to a fish fry. It didn't make much sense to him.

Matvey went back to the shore. A short distance away he saw a rock outcropping jutting out above the beach. A dirt path passed by the site. He could see that if he pitched his tarp down where the rocks met the beach he wouldn't be observed by the security guards when they patrolled.

As he prepared to sleep, pulling the tarp over his chest, he looked out at Clifton Bay. There were over a dozen sailboats with lights at the top of their masts making it look like a field of low, bright stars. He wondered which one was *Sunshine* and how the children might be doing. He would miss them. His sleep was fitful throughout the night. He woke at dawn when he heard footsteps and voices on the trail above his hideout.

Peeking up from the rocky shore, he saw walkers out in the park for early morning exercise. He was relieved it was not the park security men. Because it was still early, Matvey decided he should wait until more people were at the park. If he was to blend in with tourists, there must be tourists to blend in with. He sat on the beach looking out to the horizon, watching the boats swing and sway on their anchors. Some departed, setting their sails and disappearing into the distance. While he waited, he munched on an energy bar and drank a bottle of water from his knapsack.

On *Sunshine*, Matvey was gone when the children stirred in the morning. They were inconsolable. "Why did he go away? He could stay with us and help you and Mom sail the boat. He was our friend. We didn't even get to say goodbye."

While Linda and Mike were whining and crying, Judy tried to comfort them by explaining, "Matvey had to go because he had business to do. He needed to get back to his family who are probably waiting for him in the USA by now."

Linda and Mike seemed to calm down but they were sad for the rest of the day. In an attempt to cheer them up, Pat added, "You know, maybe you will see him again. Life has a funny way of unexpected coincidences happening. Don't give up hope and just pray he will be OK."

Mike asked, "What's a co-in-sedints?"

While he was trying to explain what coincidence meant, Pat was thinking to himself that Matvey would probably never know how beloved he was by the kids. Pat realized that he, too, missed having Matvey aboard.

As Matvey looked out across the bay at *Sunshine*, he thought about how much he was missing the family who rescued him and saved his life. To himself, he thought, "Now I must turn the page and get on with my life. I hope I can one day meet them again and give them a proper thank you." With that, he stood.

From Matvey's hideout in the rocks, he heard a loud voice of authority speaking to a group of people. It seemed to be a tour.

The leader was in a uniform and a dozen people were walking behind her. They stopped just above his position.

"This is the view of Clifton Bay. That island out there is Goulding Cay. Some believe there is pirate gold hidden on the island. Many have looked but no treasure has been found. At least nobody has admitted finding the gold on Goulding." She chuckled and continued, "Let's move on to the remains of the first plantation house built here. It was built by a planter named Johnston. This entire area of Clifton Heritage National Park was later owned by William Whylly. He bought the land after he fled North Carolina following the American War of Independence. He was one of many Loyalists who came to The Bahamas. The colonial planters brought their slaves…."

The narrative faded as the group moved on, so he quickly folded and stashed his tarp in his knapsack in case he needed it again. Then he hurried to catch up to the group.

When the leader turned to continue her story, she noticed Matvey. "Oh, are you joining our group? I didn't see you on the trail, but please join us." Matvey nodded and tried to say in his best English, "I am a tourist from España. Oh, I mean, Spain." When Matvey was under pressure, his English pronunciation was worse and his Spanish accent became more prominent. But, the tour leader did not seem to care.

The tour continued through Clifton Heritage Park. Matvey listened attentively to see how much he could learn about where he was. None of the tourists seemed very friendly. They were older Americans on a tour from a cruise ship. They were weary from walking and most were moving slowly. The leader needed to stop frequently to let stragglers catch up. Matvey realized that he did not fit in with this group of seniors so he tried to stay at the back to avoid attracting any attention to himself.

As they looped back to the visitor entrance, a bus was waiting to take the visitors back to the cruise port. Matvey followed along like he was part of the group. Getting on the bus last, the driver snapped at Matvey, "Hey, what do you think you are doing, man?"

Matvey had been caught in his ruse. He was starting to back out of the bus when the driver laughed, "Go ahead. Get on. But this ain't no taxi!"

Matvey paused again trying to decide whether to get off or on. The driver continued, "You look like you could use a ride, so get on!"

On the way back to the cruise port, Matvey watched out the window, keenly observing the landscape, the people, and the buildings. Everything looked new and well maintained, not at all like Cuba where time and the U.S. embargo were crumbling the people and buildings. He noticed the cars were driving on the opposite side of the road, unlike in Cuba where drivers kept right. Here they were on the left. It was confusing.

As they got closer to Nassau, the bus slowed in the increasing traffic. He noticed more and more people were on the street and there were many cars, just like the Florida Keys and Key West. He noticed that the ocean was not as visible as it was from the Malecón in Havana, but it was the same familiar waters as the Keys and the beach he grew up on at Girón. He liked this place and hoped he could find a way to disappear into the community.

The bus turned the corner passing big fancy hotels with landscaped grounds and a golf course. Then, there was a fort on the right side of the road high up on a bluff. A sign pointed to

"Fort Charlotte." Tourists were walking up the hill toward the old fortress.

The bus drove through a crowded one-way street lined with small shops and packed with shoppers. Then the driver turned into the cruise ship terminal and stopped. Although Matvey was the first to exit the bus, he turned and waited to help the old people disembark. As he did, he noticed they all had necklaces with tags. He figured out that the tags must be badges that passengers needed to get back on the ship. He watched as the group ambled away, back to the cruise terminal. Matvey decided to walk back to the crowded street. By this time he was hungry.

Passing by the Colonial Hilton Hotel he noticed a familiar name across the street. He crossed the street and walked past the McDonald's that looked out of place with the local architecture. Instead, he walked into the restaurant a few doors down the street with a sign outside that said, "Carlos Cuban Cafe."

The restaurant was in a storefront in an old traditional building. Posters taped in the window said "Help Wanted," in English and subtitled in Spanish. He thought, "This will work. I have some money. I will eat and they will have espresso!"

As Matvey entered he was met by a hostess. She was not Cuban. She was an English-speaking Bahamian. She greeted him warmly, "Sir, welcome. May I help?"

Matvey said, "I would like to order an espresso and empanadas."

"Of course, follow me." She guided him to a table, handing him a menu and saying, "A server will be right with you. I will get you water."

Matvey didn't quite know how to act in a restaurant like this in this new country. He was on his own, in a new place, but, in a way, it was familiar. The smells of Cuban food reminded him of home.

A beautiful young lady came to his table. Wearing a white golf shirt under a black vest, embroidered with the restaurant name, and a thigh-high black skirt, she smiled as she placed tableware and a napkin on his table.

Matvey spoke in Spanish to her before she could even ask for his order. "¿Eres Cubana? Are you Cuban?"

The pretty waitress shook her head no and smiled brightly. "¡Soy Colombiana! I only work at a Cuban restaurant!" Chuckling, she asked in Spanish, "May I take your order?"

Matvey asked for a café con leche and empanadas.

"What kind would you like? Carne de res? Pollo? Cerdo? They all come with frijoles negros Cubanos y arroz." She was waiting for his answer with her order book and pen in hand.

Matvey decided on beef. It was a premium meat in Cuba, mostly not available and, when it was, it was expensive. He would treat himself. He was hungry and a little tired. He had money, more than a hundred U.S., that would pay the charges.

When the waitress returned with his order, they had an active conversation. While sipping his coffee, Matvey learned her name was Cali, like the city in Columbia. She had spent two years in Havana and loved the old city. Her aunt was married to the owner of Carlos Cuban Cafe and she lived with them over the restaurant.

"I see in the window the sign for help wanted. Maybe there is a job here for me?" Matvey inquired.

Cali smiled. "Maybe you should eat first and see if you like our food. I will ask my uncle if he wants to talk with you when you are finished."

Walking away, she stopped and turned back, addressing Matvey, "You don't look like a Cuban, but you speak with a Cuban accent. What is your name? Where are you from?"

With a mouth full of empanada Matvey slurred his answer.

"My name is Matvey Valdez Descon. I am Cuban, from near Cienfuegos!"

"OK, no problem. I will tell my uncle." With an over-the-shoulder glance, she walked back into the kitchen, musing, "That is one handsome Cuban man! Wonder what his story is."

After eating his lunch, Matvey waited at his table. Cali returned, followed by a short middle-aged man. There was no doubt he was Cuban.

"¡Hola Matvey! My niece tells me you asked about a job. My name is Carlos. I am the owner. What can you do? Have you worked at a restaurant?"

"Yes sir. I grew up in a resort in Cuba. I worked everywhere from the hotel to the kitchens. I can do many jobs."

"We need a server and a dishwasher. Could you do either of these jobs?"

"¡Sí, sí, sí! I can do both! I will work hard." Then Matvey shared more than he needed to, "I am just arrived in Bahamas. I came on a boat."

Carlos raised an eyebrow, "Were you trafficked from Cuba?"

Matvey realized he had opened a can of worms. "No, No, No. I came from Florida with my friends on their sailboat. I am living in Key West in Florida."

Carlos said, "Good. Where is your passport?"

Lying, he offered, "I don't have one yet. I am not a citizen. But, I have Estados Unidos immigration papers and a work permit. But they are on the boat and my friends have left." He paused, then added, "I can try to contact them where they are going."

With that explanation, Carlos felt it was a safe bet to hire him, temporarily at least. He figured the worst thing that could happen would be this man being caught by immigration and deported. Maybe he could get his U.S. documents and apply for a Bahamas work permit at some point in the future.

"OK, young Matvey, we will try you. Where do you live?"

"I don't have a place now. I just arrive. All my things are on the boat too. I am desperate."

Carlos looked hard at him. "Are you in trouble? This seems suspicious!"

"No, No. I assure you, I am not a problem, only in a bad situation. I just want to get a job and work my way back to Florida. It was a mistake for me to go on the sailboat!"

While Carlos suspected there was more to Matvey's story than he was being told, he wanted to help out a fellow Cuban. Years ago, when he arrived in The Bahamas, he was in a desperate situation himself. Then there was the fact that the restaurant was short-staffed and this guy could help. The arrangement would be mutually beneficial.

"OK. My wife will arrange a place for you to stay, and we can get you some clothes including a waiter's uniform. You will start tonight!"

NINE

As the days passed, Matvey settled into his new job. He liked working in the cafe and he liked Carlos and Cali. He focused on doing his job well, dedicating himself to being perfect at whatever task he was assigned. He was ready and willing to assist in any way he could.

At first, he struggled with taking orders from the customers because his English fluency was a little lacking. But, because they were not at all familiar with the Spanish names on the Cuban menu, beyond a Cuban sandwich, many local and tourist customers just pointed to the photos on the menu. Pointing was just easier.

Carlos was impressed with how well Matvey was performing his job. Yet, he was watchful over his pretty niece and protective of her getting the attention of this new, handsome, young coworker.

One night, at the close of business, Carlos assembled the restaurant staff to announce a special catering engagement they had for an upcoming weekend. "This is an important job for us.

We will be in charge of all the food and service at a pig roast on a private compound on the south side of the island, down near Clifton Park. I will need all of you to help prepare for this big event.

"The Cuban Hog Roast is an annual fundraising party for the Bahamas Conservation Foundation. A prominent Bahamian opens his estate to welcome an "A-list" group of people from the nation as well as friends from abroad. Invitations to this unique social event are prized and a sign of social status. Just so you know, the Bahamas Conservation Foundation is in charge of the country's national parks and an important advocate for the environment.

"So, it goes without saying that we must do a good job for this event. This is a big deal for us! It will mean much business for us in the future, not just from the Foundation, but from the people who come to the party, too."

As the date of the event approached, Carlos reviewed the menu and made assignments to the staff. It took a week to prepare. Carlos and his wife, Carmen, secured the supplies and hired a few local Cubans to assist with the traditional roasting of the hogs. Tablecloths, glassware, plates, and decorations were gathered by the restaurant staff.

On the day of the party, the staff had their specific jobs for setting up. Carlos and Carmen wanted to be sure everything was perfect. Staff were instructed to be particularly attentive to serving the guests. Servers and busboys were told to be invisible to the prominent attendees. Any mess or empty glass or plate was to be removed quickly. Any request was to be graciously fulfilled.

Carmen reminded the workers, "These are VIPs–Very Important People! Do not speak unless they talk to you first. Then, do what they ask, quickly and professionally. Our company reputation depends on you! Let's all work together and do a great job!"

On the day of the event, everything was ready to go after a hard day's preparation. The bars were set up. Tents and tables were in place. Sound checks for the bands were completed. Attendants were waiting to direct parking and escort the guests from the parking area to the event site in golf carts.

After changing into their formal uniforms, Carlos Cuban Cafe workers waited patiently for the first guest to arrive. The sponsoring organization's staff would be in charge of directing parking, orienting the attendees and guiding them to their tables.

Finally, a few minutes after the event was scheduled to start, guests started arriving. Their dress was tropical-casual mixed with Cuban-themed outfits. Gentlemen were wearing silk guayaberas or white sport coats over colorful Hawaiian shirts. Ladies were in their finest sundresses, with a few wearing glamorous, sparkling party attire. Any lady wearing heels had a difficult time walking the sandy paths at the venue.

Leading members of Parliament from both political parties mingled with the guests. Politics was suspended for this important fundraising event. Both political parties wanted to be seen as supportive of the national parks and environment of The Bahamas.

Music started to play. Waves of sound from the bell-like steel drum ensemble drifted through the mango tree orchard. Promptly at sunset, the Bahamian band struck up the national anthem of The Bahamas. Out of respect, guests stopped talking and stood quietly.

At the conclusion of the national song, a procession of Junkanoo crewe, outrageously garbed in creative, brightly-colored, sparkling and bespangled costumes, snaked through the crowd, clinking cowbells and dancing to steel drum music and brass horns. All eyes were on the pageantry. The entrance march was followed by a popular traditional West Indies tune, "Brown Girl in the Ring". The featured entertainment, a Cuban band, followed behind the Junkanoo group and took their positions on the stage as the Bahamian steel pan band departed.

A clinking wine glass held close to the microphone quieted the crowd and drew attention to the main stage. The honorary chairperson for the fundraiser, the wife of the Governor General, welcomed the attendees and recognized dignitaries and politicians from the current Progressive Liberal Party government and the minority Free National Movement party. She acknowledged the presence of Dr. António Arias Montañez, the Cuban Ambassador to The Bahamas. This risked offending prominent local Cubans who were major donors to the Foundation, but the Cuban-Bahamians graciously put aside long-standing political differences in the spirit of the environmental cause.

Chairperson Mrs. Angela Mackey continued, "Señors y Señoras, my friends!" The audience applauded and whistled enthusiastically. Mrs. Mackey bowed, acknowledging the accolades, and continued, "The environment of our Bahama-land is so important. But, we need to remember our beloved archipelago shares a border, not by land, but by sea - the Atlantic - with the U.S. and our Caribbean neighbors. We are not separated by the sea; we are all connected by the ocean and the sky, and even by the birds that pass through our islands. Tonight, we celebrate our natural connections. Tonight, enjoy Cuban food and culture. And, please be generous in your contributions to the organization that helps protect our beautiful land, reefs, and beaches – the Bahamas Conservation Foundation! Now, enjoy the delicious food and the talented entertainment. Enjoy!"

At her conclusion, the band started playing a fast-tempo Cuban rendition of a popular salsa tune, getting the party underway. As the music played on and the beer, wine, and rum flowed, the evening sun disappeared and the trees were illuminated with colorful spotlights and myriad twinkling LEDs strung among the branches and palm fronds. Cali wandered through the audience, distributing mojitos to the guests. Matvey followed, collecting empty glasses.

Guests were enjoying the camaraderie of their peers on this balmy evening. Some lounged to listen to the band and watch the couples dancing on the temporary dance floor. Men, and some women, retreated to a large deck at the beach shore to smoke Cuban cigars in the smoking lounge set up away from the main event. Casual as well as deep conversations were conducted at the beautifully decorated tables.

Between songs, Mrs. Mackey announced dinner was ready to be served. The band resumed its setlist. Carlos made a flamboyant presentation while bringing the roasted pigs to the carving tables. His cooks, dressed in tall white chef's hats, began carving portions for guests. Waiters were assisting with the delivery of food and drinks and clearing tables. Guests were dancing in the tents and on the temporary dance floors set up in front of the band.

Matvey was astounded at the casual elegance of the party. Everyone there was wealthy. He did not recognize any of the celebrities who were present when Cali pointed them out to him. Cali explained that many of the guests lived in several nearby gated communities that separated these people from ordinary Bahamians or the tourist population.

As the festivities continued, the party became a little less active. People were seated at their tables, engaged in conversation, or listening to the band. Some were still dancing. As the party was winding down, the staff was less involved in serving and clearing so Matvey and Cali took a break for a minute to watch the band.

During one particularly lively tune, Matvey grabbed Cali by the arm and put his hand on her waist as he started to dance on the sandy ground. He thought no one could see because they were in the shadows off to the side of the stage. Cali was a good dancer. They moved well together.

But, their dance did not go unnoticed. A shapely woman on the dance floor stopped dancing with her partner and walked over to interrupt Matvey and Cali's dance. She was tall and svelte, walking with distinct self-assured confidence. Her costume for the evening was a chiffon wrap over a tropical imprint of scarlet birds, leaving her toned midriff exposed.

She turned to Cali, "May I cut in and take this handsome man to dance with me?" She placed her hand on Matvey's shoulder. The expression on Call's face was somewhere between shock and awe. Her knees seemed to buckle a bit.

Cali stammered, "Yes, yes of course! Miss Ritiki...Miss Caroni. Oh, I am such a big fan!" The lady smiled a thank you.

Matvey was a little dumbfounded. This lady who was taking his hand must be very important for Cali to react with such deference. He noticed that she had the presence of a celebrity, exuding a charismatic aura and mysterious smile.

Miss Caroni took Matvey's hand and led him to the dance floor. He remembered Carmen's warning not to engage with guests, but this woman was leading him to the dance floor. A little panicked at being within sight of all of the guests, he thought to himself, "What choice do I have? Carmen said to 'Do what they ask and act professional.'"

Once on the dance floor, she started to lead. Matvey followed for a step or two and then his ingrained choreography took over and he led. The two were magical, well-matched physical specimens.

Soon, the dance floor was all theirs. They were surrounded by an audience of bystanders observing two obvious professionals and clapping in rhythm to the music.

It was an unlikely pairing, the sleek celebrity Miss Caroni and an unknown waiter. Their dancing rekindled the waning energy of the party, drawing a crowd of observers. They were applauded at the end of each number as the celebrity and the waiter danced through several songs. Matvey was in his element and, after recovering from the initial embarrassment of being singled out, he was obviously enjoying himself.

Carlos and Carmen were beside themselves. They worried that this transgression of the lines separating the servers from the served was being breached by Matvey. It would be impossible to get Matvey off the dance stage without making a scene. They would just have to wait to see how angry the organizers would be.

Carlos whispered to Carmen, "I knew we should not have hired him. When this is over, we will fire him and put him out on the street!"

Carmen was distressed, lamenting, "We will never be asked to do this pig roast again!"

Eventually, Matvey and Ritiki took their bows. Even the band stood and applauded their performance. Ritiki Caroni told Matvey, "You dance so well! Where did you learn to dance like that?"

"Señorita, I grew up in Cuba. My mother was a professional dancer trained at the National Ballet. She taught me before she died. We used to dance together for the guests at a resort."

"Oh, I'm so sorry, but she left you with quite a talent. Thank you for dancing with me!" As an afterthought, she said, "I hope you will not be in trouble with your boss." She noted his expression change to dread when she mentioned his boss.

When Miss Caroni saw Matvey and started to dance with him she didn't even imagine that a server might not be allowed to interact with the guests. She acted on the impulse to ask someone to dance who was obviously more skilled at dancing than her discarded dance partner.

Now that they had stopped dancing, she realized the potential problem her breach of etiquette might cause for this fetching Cuban. "Introduce me to your employers," she said with authority.

Matvey took her to where Carmen and Carlos were standing behind the remnants of the pig.

"Let me introduce myself. I am Ritiki Boca de Caroni. I took your employee, err, I don't even know his name?"

Matvey spoke up, "Matvey, Matvey Valdez Descon."

She nodded and continued, "Please don't be angry. I took Matvey to be my partner to dance with me. It is not his fault. But you can see he is a wonderful dancer and, corrupting a line from a popular song, *these lips don't lie!*" She smiled.

Carmen and Carlos were gracious in the face of one of New Providence's most celebrated residents. Ritiki was an international sensation, at least in the Caribbean. "Oh, no problem Miss Caroni. He will not be in trouble." Carlos hid his inner anger. Miss Caroni curtsied and departed to rejoin her contingent.

The head organizer of the pig roast pushed his way through the guests as he came toward Carlos, Carmen, and Matvey who were talking about meeting Miss Ritiki Caroni, a famous star. The organizer broke into their conversation excitedly, as he exclaimed, "That was fabulous! Why didn't you tell me you had such talent on your team? Next year..."

That's all Carlos had to hear to evaporate any anger with Matvey. He immediately took pride in having Matvey on his crew.

Guests trickled off. A few were stumbling to waiting limousines. All in all, the fundraiser was a huge success. Cleaning up and packing the equipment would go well into the early hours of the morning. There would be no music, only the gentle breeze blowing from the southern shore. Back at the restaurant, the rest of the cleaning up could wait until tomorrow. For tonight, the successful accomplishment was enough.

TEN

For the next week, conversation at the cafe was abuzz with the accidental interaction Matvey had with Ritiki. His coworkers were quick to clue him in on how big a star in the Caribbean she was. He had never heard of Ritiki when he was in Cuba or even when he lived in the Florida Keys. But clearly, she was well known and admired in The Bahamas.

Matvey continued working hard at his job, doing whatever position needed filling, be it waiter, busboy, or dishwasher. In the days following the pig roast, Carlos and Carmen didn't speak to him about the incident with the singer/dancer star. They only complimented him, along with the other staff, as they distributed a generous gratuity from the Foundation for the great food and flawless service at the hog roast.

About a week after the successful catering job, as he waited on tables, Matvey saw two men come into the restaurant. They were not dressed as tourists or locals but in sleek suits with silk t-shirts, and gold chain necklaces. They spoke with the hostess and then Carlos. Carlos led the two men to where Matvey was standing.

"Matvey, these two gentlemen would like to speak with you. It will be OK if you sit at a table for a few minutes. Cali will take your tables."

This was very unusual. Matvey was a little anxious about what these two well-dressed men might want with him. Were they from the government? Which government – Cuba or The Bahamas? Were they police? Or maybe they were from Immigration? He had no idea. The last time two men dressed in suits spoke with him, he ended up abducted and on a boat bound for Cuba.

The shorter one took off his dark sunglasses and laid the pair on the table. He gestured to Matvey to sit down in one of the empty seats.

"Mr. Matvey, it took us a little bit to track you down."

This only made Matvey more nervous.

The second man extended his hand, "Mr. Matvey, I am William Roque. Everyone calls me Bill. This is my associate Simon Cross. We work for Ritiki Boca de Caroni. We are part of her management team. She said she danced with you last weekend at a party."

Matvey nodded his head in affirmation.

"Miss Caroni asked us to see whether you would be interested in auditioning for a dancer job in her traveling troupe."

Matvey blinked and shook his head back and forth to clear his ears about what he was hearing. Surely, what he thought he heard could not be what they actually said. After seeing these two men wearing expensive clothes enter the cafe, he was sure he was in trouble. Trouble like when he was whisked away from Sunny's art opening by two guys who turned out to be from the Cuban government. That's how he wound up on Captain Alvero's boat with a knife at his throat. Because of two guys in suits, he wound up in the ocean.

It took only a fleeting moment for these thoughts to flash through his mind. He regained his composure, swallowed hard, blinked and said, "Sí, err, yes, I would be interested in this. She seems so nice."

"Miss Caroni thinks you might be a good prospect to be one of her backup dancers. She said you would have to learn her routines. Can you meet us at our rehearsal studio for an audition?"

Matvey said, "I am working here at this cafe and I don't have a way to get to your place, but I can try. When would this be? I'll have to ask for time off from my job."

Mr. Roque said, "We can have a car sent to pick you up. We will arrange it with your boss on when you can take off work."

With that, Mr. Roque and Mr. Cross stood, shook his hand, saying, "We will be in touch." They walked back, had a few words with Carlos, and left without ordering. After the men left, Carlos rushed to Matvey.

"Do you know who those guys are? They want to have you dance for Ritiki! I told them I would not stand in your way. You may have a chance at a new life. I didn't expect I could keep you here." He broke into a huge grin. He had an ulterior motive in helping Matvey get a job with Ritiki Caroni's troupe. He wouldn't be around the cafe to distract Cali.

ELEVEN

Matvey aced the audition with the stage manager and choreographer. He was hired and had to leave his work at the cafe immediately. Ritiki and her troupe had a rigorous concert travel schedule coming up in just a few weeks. He could see he had much to learn and not much time to learn it. He knew he would have to work hard, probably harder than at any other time in his life. But, this new life would be worth the effort.

The day following the audition, Carlos, Carmen, and Cali said goodbye to Matvey. Carmen hugged him warmly and beautiful Cali gave him a big kiss, while her uncle watched, disapprovingly. Carlos shook his hand, using both of his hands wrapped around Matvey's, as he said, "Gracias, mi amigo. You did a good job here. When you become a big star, don't forget who helped you get your footing in Nassau."

The practice rehearsals went on for two weeks. Ritiki came to one of the rehearsals and welcomed Matvey to her team. She was distant, more aloof, than she had been while they danced at the pig roast event. Perhaps it was because of the new relationship with her as a star performer and him as one of her minions. Or, maybe it was that she had been under the spell of the free-flowing Puerto Rican rum at the pig roast. Either way, Matvey could tell that she was acting differently.

Matvey learned the routines, following the choreographer's instructions to hone his dancing skills and learn the show's routines. At the second rehearsal, Mr. Cross realized that Matvey was wearing his uniform from the restaurant.

"Matvey!" Cross called out. Matvey stepped away from the troupe and approached as Mr. Cross reached into his pocket and peeled off $500 in Bahamian money from his money clip. "Get yourself something to wear to rehearsal and ditch that restaurant uniform."

Matvey looked surprised. As he noted how much cash was still in the clip, he realized he had never seen so much money all together at one time.

Cross said, "It's an advance on your first paycheck."

Cross and Roque arranged for Matvey to live in a studio apartment in the same building as many of the other performers. During his free time, he and a new friend from the troupe, Nigel, went shopping to find clothes that would replace Matvey's austere wardrobe. Walking past the tourist shops on Bay Street, Nigel was taking Matvey to stores that sold nicer clothing. Stopping at the curb, waiting to cross the busy street, Matvey looked for oncoming traffic before stepping out onto the street.

Nigel jerked Matvey's arm, yelling, "No! Stop! You trying to get killed?" A jitney bus raced by, the driver hammering on the horn. Matvey was accustomed to cars driving on the right. He had forgotten cars in the Bahamas keep left.

Excited, he exclaimed, "You save my life, Nigel! ¡Gracias! Thank you many times! I do not remember to look both ways."

"No problem, my friend. Just be careful! Remember, in the Bahamas, cars drive on the left. I won't always be there to save you!"

As they walked from store to store, picking out a shirt in one shop or pants in another, Matvey learned more about Nigel. He was a dancer from Trinidad and had known Ritiki before she was famous. But, he knew that one day she would be something special. He hitched himself to her star and had been with her during her rapid rise to becoming a major tour de force in music and dance, especially in the Caribbean islands and South America.

Nigel told Matvey, "Ritiki grew up near Port of Spain. Her father was a musician in the Venezuelan orchestra before he moved the family to Trinidad. Her mother is the daughter of a part-East Indian woman in the sugar cane area of Trinidad. Ritiki and I went to Presbyterian schools together. Her Scottish grandfather was the church preacher! She was really talented and spirited as a kid. We had a lot of fun. Then she got serious about music. As a young girl, she saw Britney Spears on TV, and from then on, she was obsessed with becoming a star, like Britney ... actually a bigger star!

"She changed her name to become the famous "Ritiki Boca de Caroni." That means the mouth of the Caroni Swamp. It's a beautiful forest, full of scarlet ibises. The only thing Ritiki loves almost as much as music is nature and her red birds!

"Now, Ritiki is all about the music business. She's made a big impact in the Caribbean, you know, from Trinidad and Venezuela, expanding into Latin-Caribbean audiences. She wants to cross over from Caribbean music to mainstream pop and be known in the U.S. I think she can do it. That's what this tour is about. She wants to perform at North American venues. After that, it's the world! She aims to be as big as Shakira or Rhianna."

Matvey said. "This is unbelievable. I only dance a few songs with her a few month ago. I had no idea she was a famous singer and dancer until my friends play her songs and show me videos. She is a very good dancer." He paused, then added, "And beautiful, too."

"You know, my friend, she must have seen something in you for all this to happen. She has no time for men, but somehow you caught her attention. Since we were kids, I've never seen her with a man, or even with a girl for that matter." He giggled and then said, "She's that focused on music and making it big."

"I am so lucky. I think my mother, in heaven, is watching out for me."

"Yes, must be. We need to get back to the apartment before our minders get upset. Strict discipline is demanded. The dancer you are replacing got drunk and missed curfew. We never saw him again."

Matvey understood. "We must be careful and keep to the rules!"

Once back in his apartment, Matvey spread his new clothes on the bed with pride. Finally, he was back to being a snappy dresser just like he had been when he was living in Cuba and dancing at Girón Beach Club Resort. He hoped he would never have to wear borrowed clothes again.

After another week of practice, it was time for Ritiki to join the rehearsals. She had been working privately with the choreographer to learn the dances and was busy with the management team planning the concert tour.

Ritiki entered the studio with an entourage of assistants. Getting ready to join her dancers, she took off her robe. She was wearing scarlet leotards with fuzzy pink leg warmers. Clapping her hands, she began speaking to the group.

"OK. OK. Thank you all for practicing without me. Please forgive me if I am rusty and get out of sync with you. Let's begin!"

They worked through each number on the setlist. There were some missteps, but none by Ritiki. She was flawless in her part. Dancers who had been working with her stand-in had to adjust to the subtleties of Ritiki's moves.

The dance team worked on each number until it was perfect or at least acceptable to the choreographer. Matvey had a significant part in the show. Ritiki had asked the choreographer to include Matvey dancing a salsa with her just before her exit at intermission and then again as the performance resumed with her spectacular re-entry to the stage. To disguise her exit and reemergence, the dance team would be dancing as a large group, along with special effects, like in a Broadway musical.

Rehearsals went on every day for one more week. After working to a recorded soundtrack, it was time for Ritiki's band to play live at each of the next few rehearsals, making the practice sessions more organic. Dancing to the same recording for each number had become easy and routine. Now, with the live band the choreography become more fluid and less consistently timed. On-the-fly adjustments would be needed as the dancers, band members, and Ritiki all worked together to make the show flawless.

After the principal show was practiced to perfection, it was time to work on the big surprise for the show planned in the stadium in Miami. They all reviewed the plan and practiced what they could. The final practice and rehearsal would be in the stadium a couple of days before the show after the special riggers set up the aerial wiring Ritiki wanted. It was going to be a risky performance, but there was no way to practice the big stunt in the Bahamas studio.

As the departure date for the first show of the tour approached, Ritiki's managers met with the troupe to go over the tour schedule and logistics. The managers presented a PowerPoint show of the tour schedule. There were photos of the venues where they would be performing. Each of the participants was given a folder with the agenda and travel information.

Mr. Cross said, "We will be making all of the arrangements for your travel and meeting with each of you individually to go over the details. Check the schedule to see when you need to be in my office. Don't be late and please bring your passports with you."

Cross repeated the schedule. "It will be at least two days between shows. Our chartered private jet will take our equipment and all of us to each site. An advance team will meet us and have transportation available at every airport. We will have security, so please have your tour badges on your person at all times or you will not be permitted to access the hotels."

Mr. Roque reminded everyone they were traveling as a group, and given the popularity of Ritiki in the places they would be visiting, he requested everyone stick together and let security keep her fans restrained. "Please be low-key, laid back, and don't go out exploring the cities we will be visiting. And especially no liaisons with local fans!"

Mr. Cross and an assistant met privately with each cast member and roadie crew worker to complete paperwork to prepare for a smooth transition into the countries they would be visiting.

Matvey was worried. So far he had avoided being asked for his passport. He knew this day would come and he had no idea how to handle the situation. The cover story he told Carlos at the cafe had worked. Mr. Cross and Mr. Roque assumed that he must be legally in The Bahamas if he was working at the restaurant. Finally, it was time for his appointment. He dawdled and didn't show up at the appointed time. He want to delay being fired and replaced for as long as possible. But Mr. Cross's assistant found him. He could put it off no longer. He would have to explain that he had no papers.

Mr. Cross was not pleased to hear that Matvey did not have a passport or any copy of his immigration status in the Florida Keys. "Matvey, this is a problem. We have invested a lot in you, through all of the rehearsals. Your part in the production is, well, significant."

Angry, he barked, "We are so close to the tour, I can't see how we can fill your part! What the hell should we do?" It was a rhetorical question. Without a passport or proper immigration paperwork, Matvey wasn't going to be able to travel.

"Please go to your quarters and wait for me to get you. I need to discuss this situation with Bill."

Matvey sat nervously on his bed waiting for Mr. Cross to summon him back. He paced the small room, watching the clock slowly tick away hours. This was probably the end of his job with the troupe. He felt helpless. He knew he would have to leave, letting down his friends, but mostly letting down Miss Caroni whom he had come to admire.

A knock at the door made him jump. He raced to answer. Mr. Cross's assistant, Marcia, was at the door asking him to come with her to meet with Mr. Cross again.

"What is happening?" Matvey asked.

Marcia replied, "I don't know. Mr. Roque and Mr. Cross have been making phone calls and left to meet with somebody about your problem. I do know they are not happy."

Mr. Roque and Mr. Cross were seated when Matvey entered the office.

Mr. Roque said, "Matvey, we have made arrangements for you to get a passport. This is a big problem and I can't emphasize that enough!" He scowled and continued, emphatically, "A BIG problem! But, fortunately, we were able to work it out. We would have appreciated you informing us of this before the last minute."

Mr. Cross sternly added, "You owe us, big time!" Pausing to let the gravity of the situation sink in, he continued, "It was not easy. We had to ask a lot of favors of many people. We met with the Cuban ambassador, Dr. António Arias Montañez. We explained your situation and glossed over that you had immigrated to the U.S. He remembered you from your dance with Ritiki at the pig roast and interceded on your behalf with the Bahamian government to expedite a work visa for The Bahamas. He also arranged for a passport to be reissued from Cuba. I hope you realize that a lot of high-powered people have pulled a lot of strings to get you *legal*. And, Miss Caroni's fame and the importance of this tour was the grease for all of this to fall into place."

Matvey was immensely relieved. He knew he owed these two men a debt he could probably never pay. He vigorously shook their hands. "¡Muchos gracias! ¡Muchos abrazos!" He was trembling and tearing up. Soon, Matvey would have a letter from the Director of Bahamas Immigration authorizing employment and a Cuban passport that would allow him to travel.

Mr. Roque said, "Now we need to take some photos for your passport. The Cuban Embassy in Nassau will email the pictures to

Havana. They will then return a passport for you on the next flight from Havana. The ambassador will deliver this to you personally. You will need to thank him for doing this for you."

Matvey combed his hair and stood in front of a blank wall for Mr. Cross to take his photo for the passport. Mr. Cross emailed the .jpg to the Cuban Embassy. In a day or two, the passport was in the secure diplomatic pouch destined for Ambassador Montañez.

The ambassador was not doing this favor for Matvey but for Ritiki. It would be good for him to have some leverage with the up-and-coming Caribbean celebrity that might be useful in the future. Matvey was a mere pawn and of no real consequence.

TWELVE

In Havana, Agent Fernández sat at his desk in a hot office. General Diego had made arrangements for him to be assigned to a desk job, manually reviewing paperwork and filing reports. It was a penalty for losing his prisoner overboard on the covert mission to Florida. The general wanted to extract punishment from Agent Oscar Fernández and Detective Inspector Carlos Costa for losing Matvey at sea. He couldn't do much to Inspector Costa because he was local law enforcement. But Agent Fernández worked for the G2 Unit of the General Directorate of Intelligence so the general could extract his pound of flesh by demoting Fernández to a mundane desk job.

Fernández spent his time going through pages of papers stacked high on his desk. Every time he thought he was making progress, a secretary would bring more documents for him to review and file. His job was to check applications for passports against the records for aliases, criminal activity, or those tagged as enemies of the Republic. If he found the application matched a record, he would alert the passport office to deny the application and perhaps refer the criminal charges to the appropriate police jurisdiction.

What a surprise it was for him to see a passport application for Matvey Valdez Descon. Fernández shuffled the form and looked at it again. He just couldn't believe what he was seeing. The pixelated photo on the copy of the application he was holding certainly looked like Matvey. Expressing his anger, he shouted aloud, "¡Mierda!" much to the dismay of the coworkers seated at desks near him. Realizing he was attracting attention, he quietly whispered to himself, "How can this scum not be at the bottom of the ocean? He must be a cat with nine lives!"

Fernández was surprised, but mostly he was angry. He blamed Matvey for his troubles. He felt Matvey disappearing into the bowels of the ocean is what got him busted down to a monotonous job from the elite position he used to hold as an investigator with the G2 Unit. It didn't matter that Captain Alvero was the one who had loosened his grip on Matvey, providing the opportunity for him to jump overboard. If Alvero had just slit his throat and he and Costa had delivered a dead body, it would have been easier to explain to General Diego what happened. And, it would have been Captain Alvero's responsibility to explain to his old friend, The General, why Matvey, the thief of the gold cross, was dead.

As he sat there staring at Matvey's application in his hands, marked "Expedite" no less, he thought, "The past is the past. I can not dwell on what did or did not happen. The issue now is that Matvey is alive. We can still bring him to pay for his crime." Fernández decided he would call Inspector Costa in Cienfuegos before alerting anyone at the G2. He waited anxiously until he was alone in the office.

When the inspector picked up the phone, before he could even say hello, Fernández was excitedly talking, almost shouting, "Costa! Costa! Listen to me! Matvey is alive. I am looking at his approved passport application!"

"What? Slow down! Fernández? Is that you? Where are you?"

"I am in an office job at the Ministry of Interior. The general made sure my life would be miserable. He was so mad he told my agency to make sure I was never allowed to do field work again. I am sitting in a hot closet-sized room going through passport papers all day, every day."

"I am very sorry my friend. The general called my boss and told him I was a bad officer and should be demoted. Fortunately, Diego isn't that popular with my chief, and I have a good work record. So you got the penalty, and I escaped without any problem. Now, tell me about Matvey! I thought, we all thought, the ocean swallowed him up!"

Fernández shouted, "No! He is alive!" Costa grunted. Fernández went on to say, "It looks like there was a special request from the Cuban Ambassador in The Bahamas to secure a new passport for Matvey. I am looking at a bad copy of the application, but it fits with him - age, height, and even the blurry photo."

Costa questioned, "How could that happen? You are sure the photo is a match? Could this be a coincidence or is somebody using his name? I think he is long dead."

Fernández argued, "No! It's him! His blonde hair and green eyes show through the copy of a copy I have in front of me. Everything looks like a match. How could he get the ambassador to help him? I have no thought about how he could be connected to the ambassador."

"Let's think this through. Maybe you should try to get more information from the embassy in Nassau."

"You are the only person I contacted. Because of what we went through, I knew you would want to know. Now, I need to figure out what to do. I am in such a menial job I need to be careful who I ask about this. But, I would bet that General Diego doesn't know! When I know more I will call you back."

Fernández set Matvey's application aside, hiding it in his desk drawer. He did not want to attract the attention of his autocratic supervisor. Later, when he was alone, he used the computer to find the contact information for the Cuban Embassy in Nassau.

Using his personal cell phone, he placed a call to the embassy. Reprising his former status, he started, "Hello. This is Investigator Oscar Fernández with the G2 Unit of the Directorate of Intelligence. I would like to speak to someone about a passport application I am investigating."

After a few minutes, he was connected to a deputy ambassador. Fernández relayed, "I am looking at a passport that has been issued to Matvey Valdez Descon at the special request of Ambassador Montañez. Can you provide any clarification on this?"

"Yes sir, I assisted in getting a passport expedited for this young Cuban. He is a performer in a troupe of the Trinidad singer Ritiki Boca de Caroni. He said he lost his passport. He needed a new one to travel on the upcoming big concert tour the band has. Is there a problem?"

"The problem is that the passport has been issued before I could review the applicant's history. He has an arrest warrant for the theft of national artifacts in Cuba. He escaped capture last year and was presumed dead. Now it is evident that he is not dead and, with the passport, he can travel again and further evade arrest."

"Oh my. I can see the problem. I will discuss this with Ambassador Montañez and call you back. How can I reach you?"

Fernández gave the assistant ambassador his private cell number. He wanted to keep his investigation secret until he had more facts and could devise a plan. While he waited, he searched the Internet to find information on Ritiki Boca de Caroni and looked for photos of Matvey.

Fernández waited for two days before his patience for getting a return call expired. He could wait no longer. He phoned the deputy ambassador again.

Once she was on the phone, she was guarded in her conversation. "I'm sorry Mr. Fernández, but the passport has already been given to Mr. Descon. The Ambassador is not anxious to have any further problem with this because we have asked special favors of the Bahamians and it will be embarrassing for our relations if it is found that we helped a criminal. Perhaps you can let this go and pursue another way to interdict Mr. Descon, preferably in another country, and not too soon. Can I assist in any other way?"

It was clear that the Cuban embassy did not want to get involved with anything that exposed their mistake of not vetting Matvey's background before getting him a passport. Fernández called Costa to let him know he had run into a dead end.

Costa asked, "Can we meet somewhere to discuss what to do? We could meet in Havana when I come to visit my family this weekend. Is that OK with you?"

Fernández agreed. "Until we can meet and create a plan, I'll sit on the application and not tell superiors that a passport has already been issued to a criminal."

On the weekend, the two men met at the plaza near the Malecón. Sitting on a bench they bemoaned the unfair penalty imposed on Fernández for a mistake that was not his fault. Then, Fernández relayed the information about why the ambassador helped Matvey get a new passport.

Costa said, "I'm lucky to not have any repercussion from his escape, but then I'm more out of Diego's sphere of influence. I'm not happy he escaped. But, mostly I'm curious about how he could have gotten away from us. It's a miracle he survived!"

Pausing for a moment of thought, he then continued, "Maybe we should let this go. If the ambassador will be embarrassed by his mistake being exposed, it may only get us in more trouble."

Fernández barked, "No! We need to follow up on this. He got away from us and I think we should follow the lead to redeem ourselves." It was a matter of pride for Fernández to have Matvey face justice. He hoped he could regain his former life if he could bring Matvey back to Cuba.

"How? If the ambassador isn't interested, how can we do anything? You are not in a high-level position anymore. If we report it to your superiors, it will probably only make problems for the ambassador. How would that get Matvey back to Cuba and you back in the field? It might even put *you* in more hot water because you would have a general *and* an ambassador pissed at you."

Fernández was silent for a minute. Then he said, "I have an idea. We can talk to Captain Alvero and tell him Matvey is alive. If he will introduce us to meet with General Diego, maybe we can convince him to give us another opportunity to try – no, to succeed this time! This time we will not involve Alvero in the operation. He's the one who let Matvey jump and I've been the one paying for his mistake."

Costa thought about Fernández's suggestion. "Yes we might try, but it is risky. Alvero is full of rage, and I don't know if we can trust him to be discreet. But, my friend, I hate for you to be at a desk instead of on the street. It is worth a try."

"I have thought about how this might work. If General Diego can persuade Ambassador Montañez to help, we can arrive in Nassau on a tourist visa and wait for Matvey to return from the concert tour. I'll bet that the ambassador will agree to help to keep his mistake from being revealed. I looked up the schedule on the Internet so we would know when to get to Nassau. Then we follow him for a day or two to make certain the guy who got the passport is the right man, is actually Matvey. Once we are sure, we present an arrest warrant and extradition request to the Royal Bahamas Police Force. When he is arrested, it will be easy to bring Matvey back on a commercial airline from Nassau to Cuba."

Costa agreed, "That will work. The apprehension of a criminal would be official, not like being undercover like we had to be in Key West."

"We must convince General Diego to give us another chance!"

When Fernández called him, Captain Alvero was outraged to learn Matvey was alive. He tried to contain his temper, but the death of his family still weighed heavily on his mind. In addition to his sorrow, he also felt guilty and angry with himself for losing Matvey when the captive had been secured on his boat.

Fernández convinced Alvero that he should not be involved in another attempt to bring Matvey to justice, not only for the crimes the government wanted him for but for the revenge Alvero sought. Fernández explained, "You are too close and emotionally involved. That's what makes mistakes happen. Capturing Matvey this time will not need to be as secret as the operation in Key West was. Cuba has relations with The Bahamas that will allow us to be in the country legally. You will not need to take *La Luna Grande*, with us hiding on board, to The Bahamas. What we need from you is to use your friendship with General Diego."

The captain was more than happy to make arrangements for Fernández and Costa to meet with General Diego to propose another attempt to capture Matvey in The Bahamas. When Alvero called his powerful friend to arrange a meeting, General Diego listened. He was skeptical, but he agreed, reluctantly, to try their plan, even though he was still perturbed that Fernández and Costa had failed to bring back the antiquities thief during the risky covert operation in Key West. "I will call Ambassador Montañez."

Ambassador Antonio Montañez had the look of a diplomat, being tall and slim, with erect posture, and a little gray at his temples. Today, he was wearing a finely cut pinstripe suit with a light blue shirt and his signature tie with the colors of Cuba's flag, white, blue and red. He was deftly skillful in diplomacy, being very cautious when representing Cuba's interests while advancing relations with The Bahamas.

Being stationed in Nassau had advantages. The outpost afforded independence and autonomy. He enjoyed the social functions of the top echelon of Bahamian society. Life was easier being away from the constant political maneuvering in Havana. The principal challenge was avoiding conflict with prominent Cubans residing in The Bahamas since the Revolution. A few had deep animosity toward the Castro brothers as well as significant influence with the Bahamian prime minister.

When General Diego called Ambassador Montañez, the ambassador balked at the general's request. But, because the general had some influence in the Interior Ministry, he could not just outright reject his orders.

"General," the ambassador calmly replied, "You do not understand the difficult international consequences of your request. It seems I have made a mistake in helping a criminal get a passport without checking his record. It is also a problem that I interceded with the Bahamian government. Bahamian officials are involved in this too. If this unintentional mistake should come to light it will not go well for the trust and relations between our two countries. There are larger issues to consider, more important than catching a thief."

The general barked, "I don't care!"

With a diplomat's polite demeanor, the ambassador answered, "Oh, but I think you do. From what I understand, your agents had a clandestine operation in the Florida Keys during which your agents captured and kidnapped this young man. If that is exposed, it will create a further serious incident with the sovereignty of the United States government. If knowledge of this leaked out, it will not go well for you."

The General calmed down slightly, knowing Ambassador Montañez had hit on something that could be a problem for him. He was still worked up about Matvey having a passport when he should be in custody. He said in a heated tone, "What *can* you do to help?"

"I can offer to house your agents and assist them, very quietly, to find this man. If they get him, we can use the embassy facilities to hold him until you can send a plane to return him and your agents to Cuba. That is if you can provide a way to quietly get him back to Cuba. I must emphasize 'quietly'. We have certain protections through diplomatic immunity, but it only goes so far. Your agents will need to be acting on their own, not as a government mission."

The General realized the situation was at the discretion of the Cuban ambassador as he was without direct authority over the diplomat. He could see that any way of getting Matvey, now that he was on Bahamian soil with a valid Cuban passport, was better handled privately than being exposed to scrutiny by any government, whether Bahamas, Cuba, or the U.S.

"Fine. If that is *all* you are willing to do," the general huffed, emphasizing the word all. He followed up, stating facetiously, "Then I must accept your generous offer."

The plan to get Matvey back to Cuba officially was dead. Fernández and Costa would have to be on their own to recapture the fugitive. Neither the general nor the ambassador wanted anything to do with another failure or being implicated in any way.

THIRTEEN

The Ritiki Boca de Caroni Tour was ready to go. All of the details were settled. The advance teams were in place and had signaled that the venues were ready. The promotion of the "Scarlet Diva Tour" was going well.

Since Ritiki was already well known as an emerging artist in the Caribbean, the tour started in Trinidad. The first stop would be like a final dress rehearsal for the show. With a guarantee of a friendly audience, Ritiki could test the setlist, the band and dancer performances, and the staging, while making adjustments before the premiere event in Caracas.

Traveling on the jet was a new experience for Matvey. He sat at a window and grabbed the seat on takeoff. Then the experience became a pleasure, floating so high above the surface of the sea. As the plane turned south toward Trinidad, he flew over Clifton Bay. He could see a few sailboats anchored in the bight. He wondered if one of them might be his friends Pat and Judy and the kids aboard *Sunshine*.

Climbing higher into the sky, Matvey marveled at the wondrous puffiness of the cloud tops. Occasionally he glimpsed the ocean through breaks in the blanket of white clouds below him. He could not believe how far down it was.

Landing in Trinidad, the crew was whisked to a hotel on the Queen's Park Savannah in central Port of Spain. They drove past the large stadium where the concert would be performed in two days. Banners were stretched across the highway "Welcome home Ritiki, our Scarlet Diva." But, she was not on the tour bus. Secretly, she had flown on a private jet the day before to visit her family at her compound high in the hills near a renowned nature preserve. She would relax for a day before attending to micro-managing every detail of preparation for the first concert. She was anxious for her homecoming performance to be perfect.

The show was an eclectic combination of rhythms and sounds. She used her multicultural upbringing to imagine new compositions. Her strong charismatic personality projected a larger-than-life stage presence. She was a triple threat: multi-instrumentalist, dancer, and powerful vocalist. With her foundation in Latin music, her primary influence was the Spanish Caribbean, particularly Venezuela. The Presbyterian Church gave her exposure to traditional church hymns and black gospel. Her youth led her to Reggaeton and American Pop music hits. Her connection to the East Indian population of Trinidad tinged her music with a Hindi vibe. The power of Ritiki's music was the fusion of multiple genres. Its freshness made it distinctly original, not a regurgitation of what other performers were doing.

Ritiki was aware of how she needed to distinguish herself from other singers. She was intent on creating something new and different from what people had been hearing. Her music *was* new.

It *was* different. And, it *was* catchy. Her unique sound was taking off and getting acclaim throughout the Caribbean Basin.

Her initial success enabled her to purchase a compound in the hills overlooking Port of Spain. She was wealthy, but not super rich. She was successful, but unknown outside of her regional popularity. Ritiki carefully planned her expansion to North America and into cross-over music. Her music and the Scarlet Diva tour outweighed all of her interests except for family and brief respites in nature at her retreat.

The theatrics of her shows were as important as her music. The dancers and stage production made her concerts more of a show event than a simple concert. The nod to Bollywood music and dance moves captivated her audiences' attention. The costumes she wore, the outfits for her dancers, and the uniforms for the band were all carefully coordinated. She reserved the most exotic for herself. Ritiki was entirely immersed in her career and gambling big on this successful international tour.

Finally, after months of preparation, coordinating details, and rehearsing, she took the stage to an enthusiastic welcome by her hometown crowd. Because her music videos were broadcast on Tempo, the Caribbean music video cable channel, most concertgoers knew the lyrics of her songs by heart and sang along with her as an audience chorus. It was a bonus that Ritiki could work any crowd, making her fans feel like she was personally engaged with each one.

Matvey had a significant role in the program with two dance routines as Ritiki's partner. Just before intermission, they performed together a fantastic salsa that transitioned to a modern Afro-Cuban dance. After the intermission, when Ritiki returned to the stage,

Matvey had a key role in catching her when she leaped from a perch built high above the stage.

She was costumed in a flowing scarlet garment that sparkled in the spotlights. As Ritiki spun away from him, Matvey unwound her dress, revealing her in a form-fitting bejeweled scarlet leotard. It evoked a butterfly emerging from a cocoon.

The show culminated with Bollywood dance pageantry that was designed to be similar to a line dance, providing an opportunity for her audience to participate. Finale fireworks and a mist of fog enveloped the stage as the performers disappeared into the side wings.

A planned encore was sedate and moving. Encouraged by the overwhelming and exuberant applause, Ritiki emerged from the fog. She sat on a stool, solo, playing a Venezuelan cuatro. She performed a traditional folk ballad about a songbird who lost her wings and was rescued by her lover. Backup singers, located off-stage, gave resonance and depth to her performance. This song quieted the audience and then the cast returned for a final bow. The show was over.

Social media and Caribbean news sources were set to leverage the success of the hometown concert to promote advance sales at the subsequent tour venues. Internet videos went viral and concerts were selling out quickly. It was like Ritiki was as hot as her scarlet outfits.

In the after-party, Ritiki thanked all who had made this first show come off so well. She personally thanked Matvey for catching her in her gymnastic re-entry to the stage. "If Matvey had not caught me, I would be a songbird who lost her wings! Good night. Next show is in three days. Rest and be ready!" Ritiki then retreated to her privacy.

The next two shows went off just as well. In Caracas, Venezuela, Ritiki spoke to the crowd after the show to express her appreciation for the years her father had performed in the Venezuelan symphony. "Mi padre taught me to play the cuatro. His instrument was violin in the orchestra, but his first instrument was the cuatro, just as it was mine. Viva Venezuela!"

In Cartagena, Columbia, Ritiki invoked the name of Columbia's favorite daughter Shakira. "I am so honored to perform where Shakira got her start." In one of her own arrangements, she even covered a chorus from one of Shakira's famous hits. The audience went wild. The stadium was filled to capacity with fans who were as enthusiastic as when their national soccer team was playing at home in the Caribbean Football Union finals.

Social media was exploding. Mexico City would be the next show. Even North American media was starting to take notice. Ritiki fan clubs were starting in several U.S. cities. The management team was scurrying to keep pace with the excitement. Merchandise related to the concert tour was selling out at the venues. The team scrambled to re-order all of the DVDs, shirts, and posters and have delivery made before arriving at the next concert location.

Mexico City had the highest attendance yet. The ticket holders lined up at dawn to await early entry into the stadium. The Foro Sol baseball stadium filled with 50,000 people. Mr. Roque arranged for a large-screen TV to be set up in a park outside the venue so an overflow crowd could see a live broadcast of the concert. Attentive to connecting with the audience, Ritiki asked for a moment of silence for the spirit of Selena, the Texas Tejano singer still deeply beloved in Mexico and the hearts of Mexican-Americans.

A week later the final show would be in the huge football stadium in Miami. Up to 80,000 fans were expected. The crew knew this was an important event for Ritiki, and for them, to break out into a larger audience, greater celebrity, and the American market. A lot was riding on the success of the show. Ritiki had invested her modest fortune to fund the tour. The social media team was busy hyping the show, creating a high bar of expectation for the "Ritiki - the Scarlet Diva" concert.

The show set was erected two days before the concert in Miami. Several rehearsals were conducted including one dress rehearsal on the evening before as the final practice. Videos of the rehearsal would be used in a concert DVD and, hopefully, a cable network special. There was only one practice of the dramatic finale stunt. To keep it a secret, all media was excluded from the practice.

The evening rehearsal went well. Matvey's performance was flawless. Ritiki was pleased, yet nervous about the details.

On the day of the show, all of the performers tried to relax. Waiting was painful. The clock ticked slowly in the run up to the buses picking them up from the hotel. Once at the stadium, the excitement built. When the show started, their energy exploded into adrenaline-boosted execution of their parts.

The show began with an alto steel pan accompanied by a large drum that resonated with a deep bass. The performance started slowly. Dancers moved to the stage, synchronizing their activity to match the increasing drum beat. When Ritiki's band struck the first chord, a forceful wave of sound overflowed the stadium.

The pageantry captivated everyone's attention. The opening dance, designed to warm up the audience, was off to a good start. Then, rising up in a cloud of fog from beneath the stage, Ritiki was spotlighted, joining the dance ensemble for a minute before breaking into one of her most popular hits. The crowd was wildly enthusiastic. They were dazzled by Ritiki and her show.

Ritiki was in her prime and on her way. She danced a provocative salsa routine with Matvey before she exited in a cloud of smoke, leaving Matvey alone, acting like he was searching for her. The dance troupe joined him in a Bollywood-like number before the curtain fell. Actually, there was no curtain, but only sudden darkness to cover the dancers' departure from the stage.

During the intermission, the stadium sound system played steel drum music by a variety of Trinidad pan groups. All of the musical selections were covers of popular and familiar tunes played by the winners of the Annual National Panorama competitions. Most people had heard the steel pan play traditional calypso tunes, but they had not experienced hearing pan orchestras, with 50 drums from alto to bass, performing other musical genres. During intermission, fans, new and seasoned, rushed to the merch tables to grab a piece of Ritiki. Many felt that this show was the emergence of a music phenom. The idea had been planted, hyped, and spread by influencers and promotional advertising.

When the show resumed, the lights came on and Matvey and the other dancers reprised their dance as if they were searching for the missing Ritiki. With fireworks and a loud boom, a spotlight illuminated a figure at the top of the stadium, high above, standing on a scaffolding tower draped in neon green fabric. Ritiki spread shimmering scarlet gauze wings and leaped from her lofty perch into the open air. A collective gasp rolled through the stadium, punctuated by screams.

At that moment, air cannons simultaneously jolted the crowd. The sound of the cannons was loud enough to set off car alarms in the parking lot, in a sympathetic salute. From the air cannons, thousands of small foam bird trinkets shot out over the audience. The neon pink confetti was cut in the shape of a scarlet ibis, the national bird of Trinidad and Tobago. Each was printed with "Ritiki - The Scarlet Diva Tour" with the year and website on the opposite side. The bird souvenirs floated down to the bleachers like a gentle rain, forming clouds of crimson confetti that flickered in a kaleidoscope of colored lights. Ritiki then slowly descended on a zip line, landing in Matvey's arms. Matvey and Ritiki then began their salsa dance where they left off before the intermission.

The crowd was amazed. At first, the audience was frightened at the sight of a woman free-falling from the heights of the scaffolding. Recovering quickly they exploded in overwhelming exhilaration at the dramatic return of the show's star. People scrambled to scoop up the small souvenir birds littering the stadium as a memento of Ritiki's premier concert in North America.

The opening of the second act of the concert had everyone on their feet. Some danced in the aisles and many were swaying with each tune. If the energy of the crowd and performers could have been harnessed, it would have lit up the entire city of Miami.

The end of the show involved the entire ensemble in a powerful song and dance performance. Local extras from a high school dance class ran around the field streaming colorful banners, creating a swirl of motion that symbolized a hurricane. The backup singers' microphones were turned up for a louder chorus that harmonized with Ritiki. In another cloud of stage fog, there was an earth-shaking BOOM! Fireworks shot to the sky and the stadium went dark. The ensemble exited as Ritiki could be heard saying "Thank You" to the attendees through the stadium sound system. The performers had disappeared.

Wanting more, the stadium roared with demands for an encore. After a minute of chanting and clapping, Ritiki responded by returning to the stage, in another foggy mist. A roadie placed a stool at the center of the stage and delivered her cuatro. All of the bright stadium lights went out and she was singularly spotlighted in a bright red beam.

She started the encore by saying, "I am so grateful to you all for coming to hear me tonight and see the show we put together for you." There were shouts, whistles, and applause from the 80,000 in the stands. She continued, "I am a humble girl from Trinidad, and my roots are in Venezuela.

"There is a bird in my region called the scarlet ibis. It is our national bird, like your bald eagle. My bird, she is a bright color and my favorite. I want to sing to you a song my papa taught me when I was a child. It is about a little bird who lost her wings…I hope you like it."

The stadium quieted as she started playing. The crowd used their cell phone lights to make the stands twinkle. Her voice was clear and sweet. The ballad displayed her remarkable vocal range. The melody she played on the cuatro was amplified. Sound swirled around the stadium, creating an organic reverb. Her backup singers, off stage, sang gentle harmony on the chorus of the tune. After singing an English version, she sang in Spanish.

She rose from the stool and took a bow. The crowd was moved by the profound change of pace from the high-energy performance and applauded their approval.

Ritiki took the microphone. "I want to thank you again for coming tonight. Please show your love for the dancers and singers and band members and, of course, the road crew, who came with me to entertain you! I love you all!" She put her hands together and bowed before exiting, followed by her cast.

Soon after the applause faded, with no further encore, the concertgoers streamed out of Hard Rock Stadium, Home of the

Miami Dolphins, happy, but wanting more. That was just what Ritiki wanted - a demand for her music in South Florida. The event attracted local and some national media coverage. Soon after, the Internet would be filled with video clips and memes about this inaugural performance by a break-out artist. The gamble, using her entire net worth to advance her cross-over introduction to the U.S., would pay off and she would join the select elite celebrities known by a single name.

The after-party for the show was an emotional release for all of the cast and crew. It would go on for a couple of hours before the managers broke up the celebration. "Thank you all! This was wonderful! But, I need to remind you that we have a charter flight back to Nassau at 2 PM tomorrow. A bus will be leaving the hotel promptly at noon, so please don't oversleep and miss the bus. Good night!"

FOURTEEN

When Matvey returned to his hotel room, an amber light on the bedside phone was flashing, indicating he had messages. Not knowing how to retrieve them, he called the front desk for help. The desk clerk apologized. "I am so sorry sir, but a lady has been calling for you all night, every few minutes. She sounds desperate to get in touch with you about an urgent problem. I put her through to your phone so she could leave a message. There is even a note at the front desk for you. I can have a bellboy bring it up to your room. I'm sorry for the disturbance."

After receiving instructions from the desk clerk, Matvey accessed the messages. A woman identifying herself as Maria said she had urgent information about his safety. Her messages in both English and Spanish said, "You must not go back to Nassau! Please call me, 305-555-0981. My name is Maria. Please, this is not a prank. This is serious. I am a friend from Cuba."

The only person Matvey could think of named Maria that he knew from Cuba was Maria la Gorda. But, he thought, "Surely it cannot be the Girón woman who managed the resort where I grew up. She helped me escape when Evelyn, the art professor, hit her head and the police were coming. But, how could it be her? How could she even know where I am?"

Matvey pondered what to do. A bellboy knocked at the door and handed him a sealed envelope. Opening the note, he saw the same information as the phone messages, written in Spanish. Now, he started to think it might be a fan from the concert trying to hook up with him. That was not going to be possible because he would stay true to the rules the manager had set. Although he was tired, he thought maybe he should call the number and find out what was going on.

He stared at the room phone. The amber message light was still blinking. Yes, he would call the number.

The phone on the other end of the line rang. Then he heard a woman's voice through the handset, "¡Hola, diga me! Hello?"

"I am calling because you left messages for me at the hotel. I am Matvey Valdez Descon. Who are you and what do you want?"

"I want to help you escape being caught and returned to Cuba!"

This got Matvey's full attention. "Yes, please explain."

"My name is Maria Espinosa. I live in Hialeah but my family is from Holguin in Cuba."

Matvey thought, "Clearly, this is not Maria la Gorda."

"My cousin lives in Nassau and works at the Cuban Embassy. She took a great risk to let me know you will be in trouble if you return to Nassau. Agents of the G2 will be waiting for you when you return. She says there are two officers in Nassau to get you and take you back to Cuba. They met with the Cuban ambassador. When they find you, maybe they will have the Bahamian police arrest you."

Matvey asked, "¿Que pasa? What's going on? Is this real?"

"It wasn't easy for me to find where you and the tour are staying. I had to make many calls to many hotels all around the city. Then, I had to convince the front desk that I had an urgent message for you. Why would I go to such trouble?

"My cousin learned about this at her job. The Cuban guys have asked for the ambassador's help to have you returned to Cuba for some kind of crime. My cousin said this was not a problem for the Bahamas, but something Cuba had to do on its own."

Matvey was stunned. He gasped at the thought that his past was not behind him. "How do I know this is true?"

"Well, you can trust me or not, but only you know if you have something hanging over your head that will get you in trouble. I only have the information from my cousin. She is a fan of Ritiki and has seen the pictures of you dancing with her on the tour. The Bahamas is planning a celebration for her return and a lot of people will be waiting to meet Ritiki at the Pindling International Airport."

"How can I get back to Nassau or The Bahamas if I do not fly with the group?"

"If you have your passport, you might get on a boat to another island. I think your problem will be in Nassau. That's where the agents will be looking for you."

Matvey was puzzled about how to get from Miami to The Bahamas while avoiding the airport. Thoughts rushed through his head. "Should I stay in the U.S.? What options do I have? I can't go back to the Keys. Cuban agents may be waiting for me there. And I am part of Ritiki's crew now and I like that. I want to return to The Bahamas." It took only seconds for these thoughts to pass.

He said into the phone, "I don't know what to do."

"Matvey, you might get on a mailboat to go over. There are several of these supply ships that go out of Miami. My cousin uses them when she comes to the U.S. to shop. She doesn't like to fly.

"The boats are loaded at places along the Miami River. Maybe I can help you. My cousin, a different cousin, helps load one of them that goes to Nassau and then on to Exuma. He says sometimes they take passengers to the family islands, but only legal ones because Bahamas immigration does do inspections."

"Maria, thank you. Let me think about this and call you back if you are willing to help me."

Matvey sat on the edge of his bed. He did not like the thought that he could be captured again. The last time two guys abducted him from the street in Key West, he was lucky to escape having his throat cut and lucky the sailboat came along to save him from drowning. Fear raced up his spine.

This was an urgent situation. He decided to go to Mr. Roque's room and wake him.

"What is it? You should be in bed!" Roque gruffly chided Matvey. "It's always something with you. Just because you are a star dancer in the show, don't think you are special!"

"I am so sorry sir, but I have an emergency! I can't go back to Nassau with you and the others. My cousin Maria, here in Miami, ..mmm...called me and, uh, there is a family emergency. I need to help her." Nervously clearing his throat, he continued, "Can I have my passport? I promise to return in a day or two."

"Fine, I'm tired. I'll arrange for my assistant to get your papers together and give you your passport in the morning. You get back to Nassau on your own. We will not pay for it! That is all Mr. Matvey. Good night!" With that, Mr. Roque abruptly shut the door.

Matvey returned to his room and called Maria. "I will stay in Miami and not go with the plane to Nassau. After I get my papers from the tour manager, I will try to find the mailboat on the river to go to The Bahamas. Please tell me the name of the ship."

Maria offered, "I can help you get to the river. I will get my cousin who works there to help you. I can drive you there in the morning."

Matvey didn't sleep. He packed his bag, counted his money, and lay awake in his bed fretting about being caught and taken back to Cuba. Every hour he would get up, wet his face in the sink, and pace the hotel room before returning to bed to try to sleep.

He was nervous when it was finally time to meet the team for the breakfast buffet. He told only Nigel that he was staying. "I have an emergency here in Miami, so I won't be on the plane back. I will get there in a couple of days and see you then, my friend. Please don't tell anyone my plans, I don't want anybody to worry." He hugged Nigel and left to search for Miss Bethel, Mr. Roque's assistant, to get his passport and work permit papers.

Maria drove up to the ritzy hotel and saw Matvey standing at the curb. She was driving an older car. She honked and waved at Matvey with the enthusiasm of meeting a star. She introduced herself and opened the trunk. It was full of packages of bread. She pushed aside the bags, saying, "I deliver Cuban bread to some restaurants for a bakery. I'm going to be late today. Put your bags here in the trunk!"

They drove off from the downtown hotel. It was not far to reach the road that winds by the Miami River. Along the highway, Matvey saw areas that were full of containers, scrapyards piled high with metal junk, and warehouses selling a variety of merchandise. Street vendors were selling guineps, limes, and mangoes on each corner. Maria pulled into the driveway of a shipping company called Island Cargo Express.

Forklifts were buzzing through the parking lot, lifting pallets that were then loaded on the ship. A car was being hoisted by a crane onto the deck. A man dressed in coveralls and wearing a yellow hard hat approached Maria's car. They spoke quietly. Matvey only caught a few words, but it was obvious she was making arrangements for his passage. Trepidation raised the hair on the back of Matvey's neck. He was concerned that this might be a ruse to capture him.

Maria commanded, "You can get out. This is my cousin Ronaldo. He is married to my husband's sister's ex-husband's sister." It was of no consequence for Matvey to learn the family relationship, only that he would get on the boat, and he was not being tricked into something dangerous. He was wary of being caught again and wondered if these two could be Cuban government agents.

Ronaldo shook Matvey's hand, "Hola, ¿qué tal?" Not waiting for an answer, he continued, "Come with me. I will introduce you to the captain."

Matvey turned and raised a hand to say goodbye to Maria. He leaned into the window while saying, "Thank you for helping me! I'm not sure why you would help a stranger, but I am grateful. Thank you ... and goodbye." He turned back and followed Ronaldo.

The captain was a gruff-looking Bahamian, tall and full-chested. "This is Captain George Brown. He is the captain of this mailboat called *Pretoria*."

Captain Brown said, "Ronaldo tells me you want to sail along with us. Tell me why. Why would a snappy dresser like you want to go on an old ship across the Gulf Stream when you could fly?"

Matvey was taken aback by the direct question and stumbled to have a good answer. "Well, I'm trying to avoid some people who will be at the airport. I think they will not expect me to arrive by ship and I can get away from them. I have money, papers, and a passport. I am legal!" He handed the Captain his papers.

Brown looked over the papers and his Cuban passport. What impressed him was the letter from the Labor Minister authorizing work. "Oh, I see, family trouble! You must have a woman you are trying to get away from. I think you are OK. There is no exit paperwork here but you will have to clear immigration when you get to The Bahamas. Do you get seasick?"

"No sir. I am OK. I have been at sea before, in small boats. I can help too if you need me to do something."

"No, young man. You are along for the ride. You will be in a guest cabin and eat with me and the first officer. We leave at midnight and get into Nassau at 1600 the next afternoon. For now, you can wait in the office or get on the boat and wait at the bridge. Don't get in the way. We have a lot to do before we leave."

The captain marched off, his attention now on the cargo being loaded and checking manifests.

As Ronaldo was walking away to get back to his loading tasks, Matvey inquired, "He said Nassau. I thought this was going to another island. I didn't want to go to Nassau."

"Yes, it is going to another island, but the boat stops in Nassau first. They offload cargo and then head to the Exumas to make a delivery. I even think on this trip that this boat has a stop at a small private island too, but I don't know for sure. Sorry, I must go or I will get in trouble. Good luck!"

Matvey was left alone on the tarmac of the shipping company. Standing by his bags, he thought, "Even though it will be hours before we leave, I should get on the boat to wait. In this way, I will not miss leaving with them and Cuban agents will not know where to look for me."

The hours passed as Matvey watched the scurry of activity loading crates and pallets. Another car was loaded on deck, along with two golf carts. The ship was old and rusted. Paint was peeling from every bulkhead. The interior of the bridge had cracked plastic seating and a console of gauges and monitors. From the high vantage point of the bridge, he could see the bow and the tugboats running up and down the Miami River. These old freighters were a lifeline in the supply chain for the out-islands, delivering materials and provisions on a regular weekly schedule.

As he sat and waited, he saw airplanes flying from the Miami airport. He wondered if one of them was carrying his fellow cast members back to Nassau. He wished he could be with them, as he said to himself, "It is what it is and I must do what I have to do to stay alive!"

FIFTEEN

When the charter flight arrived at Pindling International Airport in Nassau, Agents Fernández and Costa were waiting for Matvey. A huge crowd of Bahamian well-wishers and Ritiki's fans jammed the airport. Security was keeping everyone back behind barricades to protect the celebrity while they were guiding the tour cast and crew to waiting buses.

The agents did not see Matvey disembark with the other passengers. He should have been easy to recognize because he was a tall blonde man among the shorter, mostly Black, performers. Costa waited at a place where he could observe the airplane through his binoculars. Fernández went to the airport exit and elbowed his way through the crowd to watch who was getting on the chartered bus. Neither saw a hint of Matvey or anyone who was a potential match.

Costa joined Fernández at the gate after all of the passengers and crew had left the plane and the plane's and airport's doors were closed and locked.

"Did you see him?"

"No, Costa. I did not. No." Fernández was obviously unhappy that they had missed him.

A few of the crew were met by their families and did not get on the charter bus. Costa seized on the opportunity to ask one of the returning roadies if he knew where Matvey was. It was a wild shot, but the only one he had.

"Oh, he wasn't on the plane. I think he stayed in Miami. Maybe he was going to apply for a green card or something. I don't know. You should ask the manager," pointing over to the waiting bus and the manager's limousine.

Fernández mused, "¿Quizas? Perhaps he got away?"

Costa speculated, "I don't think so. He would have stood out. If you didn't see him on the stairway and I didn't see him get on the bus, he must not be with them. Maybe he came back with Ritiki? One of the workers said she probably was on a separate private jet that went to the executive terminal."

"Let's go check there!"

Fernández and Costa hurried to the special private terminal for charter jets. It had a nice lounge, with concierge help. But, there was no one in the terminal.

When they walked in, the young lady at the counter was not sure they were legitimate customers. According to her manifest, no flights in or out were expected for another few hours. Passengers didn't usually arrive in this terminal so far ahead of a flight. But, many people passed through the lounge area who were not dressed as she might expect, so she was always polite and offered assistance; no judgment, only assistance. Security could eject anyone who shouldn't be in the charter lounge.

The attendant asked, "May I help you in some way?"

Costa abruptly asked, "Did Ritiki Boca de Caroni come in here on a plane?"

"Oh, I am sorry sir, but I couldn't tell you if she has or not. Our passengers are very confidential."

From her response, Costa could not understand if Ritiki had landed yet or if the attendant just wasn't going to be helpful.

"Thank you. We are big fans! We are from Cuba and want to do a story about her for our national press. I wonder where she is. We were told to come here this morning for an exclusive interview."

"Well, in that case, I suppose there is no harm in telling you. Her charter jet landed last night, very late. I don't think she wanted to be part of the craziness at the main terminal today. Are you sure she said to meet her here? Sorry I can't be of more help."

Costa thanked her and said, "Well, my English is not so good. Maybe I didn't understand the instructions so well. Or maybe she didn't really want to talk to us. I guess I have phone calls to make! Thank you for your help."

Costa conferred with Fernández. "Do you think he's still in Miami or maybe here? Now what do we do?"

Fernández said, "Wait. We wait. We can't come back empty-handed. Diego will be very angry and he will hold us responsible. It will be even more trouble, especially for me."

Costa asked "Can we ask the embassy to see if they have a contact in Miami who can look for him? They must have some operatives there who could help."

Fernández nodded and answered, "You know we have pressed our luck with the ambassador. He only agreed to assist when General Diego bullied him. He does not want to be involved in this and demands it all be an unofficial extradition."

Fernández and Costa had a plan ready to transit Matvey back to Cuba. Now, all they needed was Matvey, the fugitive. They planned to use the embassy van to transport Matvey to the private airport terminal. An assistant ambassador had been assigned to help clear customs out of Nassau, using a "diplomatic seal" to prevent a customs inspector from looking into what they were carrying.

The day before, they had shopped at funeral homes in Nassau to purchase a casket to transport Matvey out of the country and back to Cuba. After they caught him, they would tape his mouth shut and wrap his legs and arms in plastic to keep him secure. Then they would put him in the casket and have it loaded onto the plane sent from Cuba, with a diplomatic seal, meaning the casket could leave The Bahamas and enter Cuba without being inspected.

The funeral home director had been suspicious of the two Cubans' interest in buying a casket without also purchasing the mortuary services. The impeccably dressed, distinguished, funeral home director, Mr. Pinder, had asked, "Why would you just want a casket without our excellent mortuary services? We offer many options from a natural burial to one where the deceased is entombed for eternity. Surely we could find a way to be of service to your loved one."

Fernández had tried to explain. "Oh, we are purchasing this for just in case. We have a friend who may die. We want to be ready. He is very sick," he had told the mortician in broken English.

"Oh, I see. Well, let me show you our selection of final resting places. Would you like to secure a burial plot also? We have a special place near the interment of Anna Nicole Smith, the famous

American actress. He would lie next to a beautiful woman for eternity!"

"No, muchas gracias, but no. We would take our friend back to Cuba where we have a special place for him. Maybe we might give him a burial at sea." Costa had smiled at Fernández.

They selected the least ornate casket the funeral home had. "We can keep it here for you, until you, sadly, need it," offered the funeral home director.

"No, thank you. We have a van. We will take it so we can do some special preparations to bless the casket. Our friend is a Santeria and, you know, they have some unusual customs."

That was enough for the director to quit offering his help to these two Cubans. "Fine, that will be 1,800 U.S. dollars. Will that be cash or credit?"

Astounded at the price, the two agents had looked at each other. Between them, they only had $2,000 to cover their expenses. Reluctantly, they pooled their funds and paid the director.

"Let me get you some assistance to load the casket into your van." The director had then quickly located two workers to assist Fernández and Costa as pallbearers for an empty casket. They loaded Matvey's box into the van with foreign embassy plates. As they drove off, Mr. Pinder mumbled, "Crazy Cubans!"

Fernández and Costa laughed about how cramped Matvey would be in the box. "We should drill some holes in it so he can breathe. I think the general will be happier with him alive than dead."

They both had been pleased with themselves for creating the plan, even if they were now short of funds.

SIXTEEN

Matvey sat in the cabin on the bridge of the mailboat. Although the chair he was sitting in was not comfortable, he kept dozing off, startling himself awake. Finally, he just gave in and slept. His energy had been depleted by the lack of sleep and post-concert anxiety from the night before. A loud horn blasted and he bolted up from his seat. The mailboat was casting off. The clock over the helm showed midnight. He was on his way. Tomorrow he would be in The Bahamas.

Matvey went out the cabin door to watch the shore pass by as the big boat was being maneuvered by a tug out the Miami River to Biscayne Bay. They passed under a bridge, brightly illuminated in multi-colored lights. Skyscrapers lined the banks of the river. A few small brightly-lit restaurants and bars were tucked in between the tall buildings. People were still partying at these mostly open-air clubs. Over the drone of the engines, he could hear the music beating loud rhythms. It was a relief to be moving away from the big city.

Finally reaching Biscayne Bay, the ship was under its own power, as it passed by a line of cruise ships at a terminal at Government Cut. Looking back he could see Miami's city lights, so bright that it was almost like day. The skyline faded into the horizon as they passed a steel-structure lighthouse at Fowey Rocks. With the city's sparkling lights disappearing in the distance, Matvey saw a glow over South Florida to the west and only vast darkness ahead. Stars revealed themselves as they got farther away from Miami's bright influence on the sky.

Captain George Brown was supervising his crew and checking the chartplotter for the course across the Gulf Stream to the Bahamas Bank. "Hey, you want to see where we are going?" the captain asked Matvey.

Brown pointed to a pink line on the digital screen. "This is where we are now. This is our speed. The line shows how we will go north of Bimini and on to the place where we enter the Tongue of the Ocean. Then we go straight into Nassau Harbor."

There it was again, Nassau, the place he was not keen to get to, the place where he was warned he would be in peril from the Cuban government agents. The thought even crossed his mind that his being on the boat might be a trap to catch him. Eventually, he put it out of his mind, chastising himself as being too suspicious.

Matvey asked, "Can I stay on the boat when we get to Nassau? I want to go to this place." He pointed to an island in the Exuma chain that was at the end of the plotted course.

Brown said, "I guess so, but you may want to walk on the ground after so long on a boat. There will be immigration officers meeting us at the port to check passports and customs officials to check our manifests. In Nassau, we unload some of our cargo and take on more to take to the family islands. We will be in Nassau for several hours."

Matvey felt sure he did not need to go ashore, knowing there was a chance he might be caught by the men Maria had warned him about. He decided that he would stay on the ship until they left for the Exumas.

Crossing the Gulf Stream was unlike his previous experiences on boats. Mostly the difference was in the size of the vessel. This was a ship, undulating in the large roller waves, not a small wood boat crashing into the seas of a hurricane or a sailboat with a family aboard on a calm dark night. It was not anything like his old friend Henry's fishing boat going from Key West to the Dry Tortugas when he went to secretly find his treasure of jewels and the cross of Friar Bartolomé.

As Matvey stood at the rail, reflecting on recent events, he brushed back his golden locks using his fingers as a comb. It was time for him to breathe and think. The whirlwind of events that had happened over just a few months seemed unbelievable.

He could feel the constant, vibrating drone of the engines. The breeze was refreshing and the tropical salt air was heavy on his skin. He watched the sea foam created by the bow wave as he looked out into the darkness. He could occasionally see the lights of other ships. Observing this peaceful seascape from the safe vantage of the mailboat deck disguised the dangers he had faced. Both of his narrow escapes from a watery demise were haunting memories.

Matvey turned his thoughts to the many different people he had met in the last year. "I would never have known any of these friends if I was in Cuba. There were those who rescued me from desperate situations, like Sunny, the beautiful artist who found me

119

after being shipwrecked in the hurricane that landed me in the Dry Tortugas. She was so nice to help me recover and get to Key West. Then, she introduced me to Mrs. Abrams and her hardworking caretaker Henry Forbes. Mrs. Abrams had a lot of money and a big estate, yet she gave me a job and place to live. If not for the sailboat people and their children, I would not have survived my escape from being kidnapped in Key West by those Cuban agents. Then, here in The Bahamas, Carlos took a chance and gave me a job in the cafe. Nigel saved my life from being run over by a jitney and that chance encounter with Ritiki changed my life. Like threads in a woven piece of cloth, one person led to another."

Matvey put his head in his hands. He exhaled a heavy breath, thinking, "I can't believe this. I'm on a boat because somebody I don't know said I will be in trouble if I go to Nassau. I guess I should believe it is true. Even if it is not true, I will still be safe, going in any direction the boat goes."

Captain Brown exited the bridge, interrupting Matvey's meditation.

Matvey greeted the captain, "Hola, mi Capitán." He smiled.

"Hey buddy, are you OK? You look like you've seen a ghost!"

Matvey shook his head. "I'm just thinking about where the wind will take me next. How long until we are there?"

A large cruise ship passed by the mailboat, close enough for Matvey to see the passenger cabin lights. The cruise ship was lit up like fireworks. He could see the name of the ship on the side of the hull, painted in giant letters, *Dancing Queen of the Seas*. He thought of Ritiki, "She is the dancing queen!"

The wake from the huge cruise ship caught up with the mailboat. Matvey had to step quickly to keep his balance in the pitch and yaw. He grabbed the rail to steady himself. As Matvey stumbled, Brown laughed and yelled, "You better hang on 'til you get your sea legs. You don't want to go over and be lost at sea!"

The good natured captain was grinning, but it was no joke to Matvey. He had been there, in the sea, alone and lost, not knowing if he would survive. Matvey smiled a half-hearted acknowledgment. "Yes sir, mi capitán, I will hold on."

It continued to be calm during the crossing. Matvey got a few hours of sleep in the cabin reserved for passengers. It was small but comfortable. In light of his lack of sleep the night before, the monotonous thrum of the engines, and the gentle rolling motion, he fell asleep quickly.

In the predawn twilight, the morning sky revealed pastel shades of pink and purple. As the sun came above the horizon, the sky brightened with streaks of yellow light, bathing cloud tops with golden edges. A speck of sun peaked through the line of clouds low on the horizon and then gave in to a blazing bright light directly ahead.

Standing at the starboard rail, he could see a small strip of land, with the tops of a few tall buildings rising above an island. He asked the captain, "Is that Nassau?"

"No, my friend, that is Bimini. The buildings you see are part of a new casino resort. We are not going there. We still have a long way to go to get to Nassau. Be patient, we will get there!"

Matvey wasn't anxious to arrive, only anxious to get to his final destination and escape whatever might await him in Nassau on New Providence. He wished he could get to his apartment and retrieve some things, but that could be risky.

In the daylight, Matvey could see the marine tapestry of amazing aqua blues and sea-foam greens of the crystal clear waters. The ship seemed to be floating over the bottom, gliding through the sea. A few sea creatures were visible. A sea turtle surfaced for air before quickly diving. Sharks were swimming a leisurely path looking for their next meal. A large manta ray flew through the water like a bird. He saw birds too, like the familiar magnificent frigatebirds, gliding in the sky as they searched for food. A few pelicans were diving headlong into schools of bait fish at the surface and gulls were flying overhead. He watched the water for hours, passing the time and distracting him from his anxiety.

Finally, Nassau came into view. The large hotels were visible first. Then, as they got closer, the island of New Providence transitioned from a line on the horizon to a hilly landscape. The new development of Baha Mar in the center of the city, as well as the Atlantis resort built on Paradise Island were prominent. Matvey had never seen Nassau from the water but he recognized the landmarks. He knew where he was. He was home, but he could not go home, at least not until he was safe from being caught.

The mailboat docked at the port to clear customs and offload the containers of goods and cars. Customs and immigration officials met the boat. Nobody could leave until they were processed and cleared. Some of the officials were friendly and others acted with self-important officiousness, exerting their power. Customs inspectors checked the manifests and seals of each off-loaded container.

After Matvey's passport was stamped and he was cleared, he retreated to the stern to watch the busy activity. It was hot and humid in the sun. Sitting on a large bollard, he was out of the way and mostly out of view. A crane deftly lifted and landed each pallet, container, or car and moved it from the boat to the shore. On the dock, men driving forklifts took the packages to the place where the customs inspectors were checking. After being labeled as cleared, the forklifts placed the pallets on waiting pick-ups or commercial delivery trucks. Everyone seemed well-practiced in the routine.

Captain Brown kept an eye on the operations as he caught up with Matvey at his perch on the stern deck. Captain Brown explained, "This is a weekly occurrence. New cargo that we need to deliver to the out islands is waiting at the dock to be loaded on the boat as soon as we empty this cargo.

"Once we are unloaded and reloaded for the next leg of the journey, the ship will wait at the dock to be escorted out by a tugboat tomorrow at sunrise. From Nassau, we will head back out the harbor and travel west to the north of New Providence. Then we head south to George Town on Great Exuma.

"Our departure is timed so that we arrive during daylight, so we can be off-loaded and ready to leave in the evening. Cargo loaded onto the ship at George Town is transported back to Nassau, with some of it destined to go back to the U.S. That's our normal schedule. But, on this trip, we have a special addition to the itinerary. We have a delivery of durable goods to a private island resort, Callaloo Cay Club. This cay lies farther to the south of the Exumas. It's adding two days to my passage."

Matvey had never heard of Callaloo Cay. He didn't know anything about the resort but what he did know was it was as far from Nassau as he could get on the *Pretoria*. He thought, "I'll figure out how to get back to Nassau after I get to this private island and stay awhile. Nobody will know me there and the Cubans won't have any idea where I am."

As the sun set, the loading was complete, and it was only a matter of waiting on the boat until departure in the morning. In the twilight of sunset, alone on the boat, Matvey watched people walking Bay Street to the shops and restaurants on Arawak Cay. As dusk turned to darkness, street lights came on.

Matvey was bored and hungry. He decided he would chance walking downtown along Bay Street to a take-out restaurant. He thought he might also stop at the drugstore to purchase a few items. He was familiar with the route because he had walked this stretch of road many times on his way to work at the cafe.

He knew he was taking a chance but he wasn't completely convinced that there were people from Cuba looking for him. He rationalized that Maria might have been making it all up or had bad information. Besides, he wanted to eat and get off the boat. The captain had been right about that. He persuaded himself that, if he was very careful, he would be safe.

It was dark and he had a hoodie to cover his head and shield his face. He thought, and hoped, there would be little chance that Cuban agents would be out at night. He hoped they had forgotten about him when they realized that he did not return on the plane.

As he walked, he decided to take the risk to visit his small studio apartment to get some of his things that he would like to have with him on the more remote Callaloo Cay. It was not far from Carlos Cuban Cafe where he worked when he first came to Nassau.

Once he picked up some food from a restaurant in the Arawak Fish Fry, he walked the dark streets, crossing Bay Street frequently to avoid people and illumination from the street lights. He walked up the hill and stood back to see if his apartment was secure. Carefully walking up to the second floor, he reached for the door handle. It was unlocked.

With heightened awareness, he slowly opened his door to peer inside. His apartment was in shambles. All of his things were strewn about and furniture was turned over. He retreated quickly. Bounding down the stairs, he just wanted to get away. Fortunately, no one saw him. He knew he needed to leave his things behind. He chided himself for being so naive. "Of course, the agents would come to my place to look for me. I should not have taken the chance. I need to get back to the boat."

He quickly walked past the old Fort Charlotte and cricket grounds on his way back to the port. As he passed the Arawak Fish Fry and concert stage again he noticed two figures standing by a bus stop. Matvey retreated to the shadows under the overhanging seagrape trees.

At first, Matvey wasn't sure if the two men were the Cubans looking for him. As he watched to be sure it was them, his mind was racing. "How could I be so stupid to take a chance? Maria was right. They are here for me. I should have known they would never give up. I don't know how they know I am alive, that I was not drowned in the sea."

Soon it was apparent to Matvey that these men were Fernández and Costa, the agents on the boat. Gesturing vigorously with their hands, they were fully engaged in conversation. They seemed oblivious to the people walking by. Matvey stepped further behind the seagrape trees. Then the two men started walking toward him, on their way to the Cricket Club restaurant.

Matvey was in a panic. "How can this be happening? They are coming straight at me! Do they see me? I must do something!"

Matvey pulled his parka jacket hood up higher over his head to completely cover his blonde hair. He laid down on a park bench, picking up a discarded beer bottle to dangle from one arm. He hoped they did not see him standing under the trees and that they would assume he was a drunk vagrant. They came closer, crossing the street from the restaurants on Arawak Cay to the public park. His spine tingled from the fear of being discovered. He felt his heart throbbing and he was breathing heavily. They came closer, walking on the sidewalk. As they passed he could see Fernández glance at him. He held his breath, frozen in fear. With his face in the shadows and one arm over his head, he wasn't sure that he wasn't recognized, because Fernández kept looking.

Fernández said to Costa, "Keep an eye on that drunk. Nassau is not as safe as Havana." They walked on.

It seemed like forever before Matvey felt safe enough to sit up. He slowly turned to see the two men walk past the domino players on the downstairs patio of the Cricket Club. They entered the narrow stairway that went up to the pub and open-deck dining area overlooking the cricket playing field. Teams were practicing their skills under the bright field floodlights. The area was streaming with light that deeply contrasted bright areas with dark shadows. When Matvey saw the two men seated on the deck, he felt it was safe to make his retreat back to the mailboat. He walked across the street, away from the club. He made sure he walked in the dark shadows and his head was covered by his parka hood.

It did not matter where the boat would go next. He just needed to get back on board. He was desperate to find a place far away from the populated settlements, away from Nassau, Fernández, and Costa.

The mailboat sailed with the sunrise. Matvey was relieved he escaped discovery. He shuddered at how close the two agents came when he was lying on the bus bench. Now, he was on his way, happy to see Nassau passing in the boat's wake.

Sea conditions were a little more frisky when the M/V *Pretoria* hit the deep waters of Exuma Sound. The mailboat rose and fell with the seas. It was not extremely rough, but the wind and waves were on her nose, with enough of a headwind to slow their progress by a knot or two. Arrival in George Town would be a little later than usual. When they arrived at the town landing, a crowd was waiting. Dock workers were ready to unload the cargo and would have to work into the night to complete their tasks.

Here in George Town, Matvey felt it was safer to go ashore, believing he would not be recognized in the small settlement. He had never been here before and he knew Fernández and Costa were in Nassau. A meal at a restaurant would be a good way to pass the time until the boat departed. Sitting down at a table, his back was to the door. He was facing the bay looking at a hundred sailboats and trawlers at anchor. The waitress told him that George Town was a popular place for pleasure boats that were cruising in The Bahamas.

"Boats come from all over to sail around the Exumas. This is the prettiest place in all the Bahamas," Charity said with great pride and a broad smile. "May I take your order? What would you like?"

Matvey ordered a beer and steamed grouper for dinner. With a pocketful of cash from the tour, he no longer worried about funds. He had learned a lot, quickly, about money. He even had a bank account where his tour salary was automatically deposited. This was nothing at all like his financial experience had been when he lived in Cuba. He waited for his meal, sipping a Sands beer. He was in a trance watching the boats dance on their anchors.

"Matvey!" He heard a man's voice shout from behind him and footsteps pounding the floor on their way to him. A shock ran through his body while thoughts quickly ran through his mind.

"Who could be calling out to me? I don't know anyone in George Town. But they recognize me! They know my name!"

"Hey! Matvey, is that you?" The voice yelled again. His heart was pounding in his chest. As he turned, expecting to see the Cuban agents, he was nearly knocked out of his chair by two kids.

Mike and Linda grabbed and hugged his neck. Judy and Pat followed immediately. Matvey struggled to stand with two children tightly hanging onto his torso. His chair tumbled to the deck.

Judy exclaimed, "We never expected we would see you again! How are you? You look so good!"

Pat said, "We are on the boat - right over there, behind that blue trawler motorboat. What are you doing here? How did you get here?"

More questions were asked before Matvey could answer even one. He was very happy to see his rescuers again and even more relieved that the voice calling him out was not Costa or Fernández.

"I am here on a cargo boat on my way to a private island. Then, who knows? I have had very interesting," pausing to think of the right word in English, "I guess you say 'adventures' since you left me a few months ago."

Mike and Linda begged, "Tell us, please!"

"Slow down kids. We are not in a rush. Let him get his chair off the floor. If it is okay with Matvey we can sit here with him for dinner. I promised you a restaurant tonight to celebrate." They all sat at Matvey's table, pulling a chair from an adjoining table.

Once everyone was comfortably seated, Matvey asked, "What is the celebration?"

Judy answered him, "It's the anniversary of our survival of the hurricane in the Florida Keys. We have been on the water now for a year and a half and had many adventures ourselves! But we want to hear your story!"

The kids were brown as bunnies and Pat and Judy were tanned by the sun and weathered by the wind. It appeared the cruising life was good for them.

Matvey started, "You left me at the park and the next day I made my way to Old Nassau. I got a job at a Cuban restaurant. The people I worked for had a cooking and serving job for a group that was having a big Cuban pig roast party."

Pat asked, "How long did that take? …not roasting the pig, but for you getting a job?"

Matvey smiled, "You know, it was only one night on the beach. Then I got the job at the restaurant, owned by a Cuban. He helped me a lot. When we were working at the pig roast I danced with a beautiful lady who is a singing star named Ritiki. She said I dance good and ask me to be in her show."

The entire family was amazed at his good fortune.

"I am legal now in The Bahamas, and I have money to repay you."

Pat stopped him, "Absolutely not! It is in the past, and we wanted to help you all we could at the time. We've had some good luck, too. To earn money to keep cruising, Judy and I are making custom T-shirts for the boaters we meet. She draws the pictures and I silkscreen the T-shirts. It is not a lot of money, or a lot of work for that matter, but it is enough."

Judy wanted to hear more about the singer. "Tell me more about Ritiki."

Matvey was a little nervous telling his story of dancing with Ritiki. His Cuban accent and syntax became more apparent as he answered.

"She live in The Bahamas. She is from Trinidad and a big star in the Caribbean. In the tour, we go many places. Venezuela, Columbia, Mexico, then Miami. We just finish a show in Miami that was in a big arena and was very popular. Now we are all back. I am taking a vacation to recover." He smiled. Behind the smile was the urgency of his situation that he did not want to trouble his friends with.

Linda and Mike piped in. "We missed you. We wanted to say goodbye, but Daddy said we were asleep when you left."

"I missed you, too. I miss you so much. But it is best that we have no tears when we say goodbye. We are together now and that is great!"

Dinner conversation revealed more details about Ritiki and the tour, the dancing, and the show theatrics, as well as the many places the family visited. They all stayed long after the meal was finished and the dishes were cleared, talking and catching up as friends do. Eventually, Charity came to the table. "I don't want to rush you, but we are closing now." Too soon, it was time for them to leave.

Warm hugs and a tearful goodbye ended the chance reunion. They pledged to stay in touch, but neither knew how they would. With Matvey having no set destination and the cruising family always on the move, they would just have to depend on chance to find one another again.

Matvey watched their inflatable dinghy disappear into the darkness, heading back to their sailboat. He walked back to the dock where the *M/V Pretoria* was tied. "Maybe tomorrow I will find my secret refuge."

At dawn, the mailboat cast off from the town dock on the way to Callaloo Cay. As they motored by the mooring field crowded with cruisers, Matvey looked to see if could find his friends. As the ship passed near them, he shouted out to them. It was one last goodbye.

Continuing down the Exuma island chain and passing to the east of Long Island, it would be about 130 nautical miles to a small cay near Crooked Island. This was about as out of the way in the middle of the archipelago as a place could be.

Captain Brown told his mate, "We're good out here in deep water, but we will need to be on our toes when we get close. It's a little tricky with the reefs and coral heads. I don't like those waters near Callaloo."

"Yes sir. When we get close, you can take it." The first mate laughed, "I don't want to be the one who runs your ship aground. You are the captain."

Matvey overheard the exchange, but it didn't matter to him. He was looking forward to being on a remote island far away from Nassau. It would not be long now.

The mailboat slowed as it approached the coast of Crooked Island. Captain Brown took the wheel and closely examined the chart plotter. They rounded the point and sighted the service dock at Callaloo Cay. The captain instructed his crew, "Check the tide. The depth alongside the resort's pier is a little shallow for us unless it's high tide."

Deck crew waited on the ready to secure lines when they got close. The tide was rising toward high and it looked like there would be enough depth for the boat. It was good that most of their cargo had been offloaded in George Town and they hadn't taken much on board for the return trip to Nassau. The lighter load lessened the ship's draft. Out here on the family islands, if they grounded, there was no tug to pull them off.

Brown expertly eased the unwieldy craft to the pier. The deck crew cleated the lines and moved to unload the cargo as fast as possible.

Nearly all of the Callaloo Cay Club staff was on hand to meet the ship and help offload. Several had personal items on the vessel and were anxious to get their packages. The captain was impatient. He wanted the boat unloaded and backing off before the tide switched and the water would be running out.

Matvey gathered his belongings and climbed down the side ladder to jump off onto the concrete pier. That's when he saw Clara Ruiz. He was stuck in his shoes. She was the beautiful vision of his dreams. Her flowing dark hair and gentle eyes were lovely. She walked with such poise and personality.

Clara walked up to Matvey on the pier, barking, "Who are you? What are you doing? We have no reservation for a guest!" Her forceful confrontation belied her outward appearance and his first impression. She commanded, "You must get back on the boat!"

Matvey was speechless. He had assumed that he would be visiting a place where he could stay and hide.

"I have money," pulling out a handful of cash from his wallet.

She looked him up and down, then laughed. "I don't think you have enough money for our rates! We don't take paper money, only bank transfers."

Matvey was at a loss for words and getting desperate. He defaulted to using his charm to counter her assertiveness. "I am Matvey Valdez Descon. I am here to apply to be your assistant and maybe, in time, your husband?"

Now it was Clara who was speechless. "What? I don't need an assistant! There is no job for you here. And I don't need a husband!

Get back on the boat!" She was so beautiful, even with a scowl on her face.

Matvey approached her closer. She saw he was a tall, handsome young man. His emerald eyes twinkled with a smile.

She exhaled, speaking more calmly. "Mr. Descon, let's start over. I can explain. This is a very exclusive private island resort. Our guests are very rich and have placed reservations to stay here well in advance. We are self-sufficient with all we need to operate this property and provide whatever our guests require." She paused, then corrected herself, "No, we provide whatever our guests *demand,* which is privacy and pampering. We don't need your assistance. Now get back on the boat. Please."

Matvey, noting her Spanish accent, asked, "Are you Cuban?"

Indignantly, she replied, "No way! I am from Puerto Rico!"

Matvey smiled, "I thought so. There are no girls in Cuba that are as pretty as you, but many who are as confident."

Clara smiled. "Save your charm for the Cuban girls. I'm the assistant manager here. I handle the special needs of our guests. And, I'm in charge when the manager is off-island. You don't seem to be one of our special clients!"

"But I am special! I'm a dancer, and a cook, and a waiter, and a maintenance worker, a gardener, and I can reach things on a tall shelf." Now Clara laughed.

"You see, I am a dancer, just off the Ritiki Boca de Caroni concert tour and I need a place to relax."

Clara interrupted Matvey saying, "I don't know who that is."

Continuing, in Spanish so he could more easily express himself, Matvey said, "She is a talented singer and dancer who lives in The Bahamas. I just want to visit a secluded island. This is the perfect place, and you are the perfect hostess. If I can't be a guest, please let me be a worker, at least for a little while. I will work hard and can do anything. I have papers. I am legal."

Clara was skeptical of his story. The manager was standing nearby and overheard most of the conversation. Although they were conversing mostly in Spanish, he picked up on most of it. He came up to Matvey and shook his hand, saying, "Let me introduce myself. I am Geoffrey Knowles. I'm the general manager here. Miss Ruiz is correct. We don't have a place for you here as a guest. But, if you are serious about working, we might be able to have you work here for a couple weeks … that is, if Clara approves." He looked over to her.

Clara rolled her eyes. "If you think so, it's OK with me. You are the boss."

"OK then, Mr. Descon. Get your bags on that golf cart and Miss Ruiz will show you to the temporary worker housing. We will figure out what you can do after the mailboat leaves."

Matvey rode with Clara down a sandy path to a small building with four doors. It was an awkward ride. Although they were silent, both felt something electric. Clara wasn't happy this interloper had wormed his way into a temporary job. Matvey was clearly happy to be sitting next to a beautiful woman, have a job, and be hundreds of miles of ocean away from Nassau and two guys who were intent on harming him.

Clara opened the door to one of the rooms. Inside were very simple accommodations including two single beds on opposite walls. A bathroom was located at the back of the room, with a transom window over the door and a window on the back wall, over the sink. In addition to the beds, the room was furnished with two chairs and a small round table. Each bed had a locker at the foot with some drawers. It was simple, clean, efficient, and stylishly up-to-date. Matvey thought, "I like this. I can live here." To Clara, he asked, "Do I have a roommate?" pointing to the opposite bed.

Clara said, "No, not now. The crew that stays here will be back in two weeks. After the next supply boat delivers more materials for their project, they will begin working. I think you will be our only guest worker until they return. Then you can go back to wherever it is you came from."

Matvey smiled, "Unless I can prove how important I am to help operate this resort. I have experience."

Clara rolled her eyes again. "Good day, Mr. Descon. Get yourself settled. Someone will be back to tell you where you will work after I speak with Mr. Knowles about what he has in mind for you."

Clara jumped in the golf cart and sped away. Matvey dropped his tour suitcase and carry-on day pack before walking back to the boat dock just in time to see the M/V *Pretoria* cast off her lines and start backing out away from the pier. All the materials and crates were stacked on the pier, awaiting transfer to a storage building.

Matvey ran up alongside the boat, waving at the captain, and yelled, "Thank you for the ride! Bon voyage Señor Capitán!" He gestured a salute. The captain waved him off, shaking his head over his mysterious passenger who was now at the exclusive resort.

Matvey noticed the workers loading a truck with the cargo. The man who seemed to be in charge was telling the other men what to do. Matvey offered to help.

"Sir, I am new here. I can help you with the loading."

Not knowing anything about Matvey, but guessing he was a new employee, the foreman said "Sure Buddy, dis is a lot of stuff we got to put away before we get rain. Help those guys pack up the truck."

As Matvey walked away the man shouted, "Hey man, what's your name? You call me George."

Matvey replied, "You call me Matvey."

George said, "I will call you Matt - OK?"

"OK!"

SEVENTEEN

Over the next two days, Agent Fernández and Inspector Costa wandered Nassau looking for Matvey. Showing a photo, they would ask people on the streets or in hotel lobbies who appeared to be Latin if they recognized this man. Most said no. A few said he looked like one of the dancers in Ritiki's show.

Costa and Fernández realized Matvey had some celebrity recognition because of the images appearing on the Internet. But, to the Cuban officials, it did not matter if people knew who he was. They wanted to know where he was.

Several times a day, they walked by his apartment. If nobody was around Fernández would stealthily walk up the stairs to peek inside the door. Every time he looked, he saw nothing had changed from the way they left his quarters after they had ransacked and searched it. During one of their forays to the apartment, Costa saw a neighbor arrive at the apartment next to Matvey's room. "Hola. May I ask you a question? Do you know the man in the room next to you?"

"Yes, he is a friend of mine. Actually, he is a coworker. I am a dancer in a show. So is my partner, Hector."

Hearing his name, Hector emerged from their apartment. "Hey man, you looking for Matvey? We haven't seen him since we were in Miami. I heard he was staying there. I think to immigrate from Cuba."

Costa asked, "When was this?"

Nigel spoke up, "After we finished the last show at the Hard Rock Stadium a week ago. He asked the manager for his papers so he could stay. He wasn't on the plane with the rest of us. Hey, you guys cops? Is he in trouble?"

Fernández and Costa awkwardly stumbled all over themselves to avoid admitting they were with the Cuban government. "No, no, we are just friends of his looking for him. We learned he lived here and wanted to say hello while we were visiting Nassau....as turistas."

The two agents departed in haste. "Well, maybe this effort to catch Matvey is not going to be successful. If he is in Miami, he's out of our reach, at least for now."

Hector and Nigel looked at each other with suspicious disbelief. Nigel said, "Those two were cops – Cuban cops – and definitely not Matvey's friends!" Agreeing, Hector said, "Yes. Something is not right about this so I don't know anything! Do you?" he winked.

Fernández suggested they return to the embassy and discuss the status with the deputy ambassador. Costa agreed. "We need to rethink what we are doing here and make a new plan."

At the Cuban Embassy, Fernández and Costa revealed what they had learned about Matvey to the deputy ambassador. They unloaded their frustration on the woman. She was practiced at listening and waited patiently for them to finish. Finally, after exhausting all their information, they started to repeat themselves.

She interrupted their tirade. "Gentlemen. As you know, what you are doing here is not endorsed by the ambassador. He told you that you are on your own, with very limited help. I am sympathetic to your problem and would like to help you more, but my hands are tied. If you had caught your fugitive, we were ready to help you get him out of the Bahamas, with the support of General Diego. But now you are empty-handed. What do you suggest you do now if this criminal is in Miami being protected by the gusanos, "the worms" who ran away from Cuba?"

The agents had no answer. Fernández spoke, "If I don't return with Matvey Descon my life in Cuba will be over. The general has already imposed a big penalty on me for losing him one time. He gave us a second chance to make it right. If I go back without him, I think the general will do to me what he planned for Matvey."

Costa said, "I'm ready to go home. Unlike Fernández, my job is safe and out of the general's direct influence. However angry he is with me, it will pass. I can get back to my job and my family in Cienfuegos." Looking directly at Fernández, he said, "Sorry, my friend."

The deputy ambassador understood the predicament these two agents were in. "Let me speak to Ambassador Montañez about this. Maybe he will have an idea. Why don't you walk down to the nice little Cuban Cafe for an espresso and come back in a couple hours."

Costa and Fernández left, politely thanking the deputy for her time and the support she had already provided.

When Costa and Fernández entered Carlos Cuban Cafe, Carlos saw them come in the door and immediately recognized the gait of Cuban agents. It made him bristle with resentment that Cuban interior agents would be in his place in Nassau. It was like a violation of his sovereignty. He had immigrated to The Bahamas to escape Cuba and built a new life free from the Communist government.

Smiling an artificial grin, Carlos addressed the two men. "Hola, bienvenido! It is not often I get to see compatriots from my beloved country here in my cafe! What can I get for you?" Carlos vigorously shook their hands and hugged them, patting their backs.

Fernández said, "How do you know we are Cubano?"

Laughing he answered, "I can tell! It is your walk, your way, and the look in your eyes that you need good coffee!" He introduced himself, "My name is Carlos. I am from Viñales, but I have been here in Bahamas for twenty-two years. This is my restaurant!"

He went behind the counter to start their espressos. Looking over to them while he worked he said, "What brings you to Nassau when you have Havana to enjoy?"

Costa said, "We are here as tourists. We are looking for a friend who lives here now." He then stood and held up a wrinkled photo of Matvey for Carlos to see.

Carlos replied quickly, "No – don't know him. He does not look Cuban to me! Maybe from Argentina where there are blonde Latinos?"

Costa sensed maybe there was more that Carlos was not telling. He answered too quickly, after hardly looking at the photo from meters away.

Fernández interrupted, "We think he may have been here in Nassau but is in Miami now." Costa nodded and sat to sip his small cup of robust espresso.

Carlos said, "You know there are many people who visit Nassau on the cruise ships. The street is always busy. If a Cuban visited, the first place he would go would be the McDonald's hamburger down the block. Have you tried there?"

Carlos then left the dining room, saying over his shoulder as he walked away, "Oh, excuse me, I have to go to the kitchen."

As he pushed through the swinging door to the kitchen, he jerked his head toward the dining room as he alerted the staff to not come out to the front. If they did, they were not to speak to the men drinking espresso. "They are looking for Matvey…I don't know why but it cannot be good. If asked, he was never here. You don't know him! Comprendes? Try to stay back in the kitchen as much as possible until they leave."

Carlos returned quickly with a bag of coffee in his hand as if that was the reason he went to the kitchen. He continued to engage the men in small talk, asking where in Cuba they lived, if they had families, and anything else to keep them distracted from asking more questions about Matvey. After an hour passed and they had a second espresso, they paid their bill and departed to return to the embassy. Since they were anxious to get back, Costa dismissed his suspicion that Carlos had seen, or maybe even knew, Matvey, as being oversensitive to their situation.

As they strolled back down Bay Street, the place was not as ominous in the daylight as it was when they first walked the sidewalk at night. Each searched faces in the tourist crowd for Matvey, desperately hoping that chance would favor them at the last minute and they could triumphantly return him to Cuban justice. Try as hard as they could, their strained eyes did not find their target.

At the embassy, the deputy ambassador said, "I have good news for you! Or at least I think it is good news."

Costa and Fernández looked at each other with a little hope in their eyes.

"The ambassador will meet with you. Wait here, he will be in to see you in a minute."

After a few minutes, the deputy opened the door to escort Ambassador Montañez into the meeting room.

"Gentlemen, my trusted deputy has told me of your problems. I know how frustrated you must be to not be able to accomplish your mission here in The Bahamas. But now it is time to end this pursuit."

The ambassador was anxious to have Fernández and Costa fail to capture the escapee. He dreaded the arrest would expose him in an embarrassing diplomatic faux pas. "I have a suggestion... no, an offer, for you. I understand, Inspector Costa, that you can return to Cienfuegos with minimal or no interference in your life from General Diego. But you, Agent Fernández, face some serious repercussions when you return. Does that sum it up?"

The men agreed.

"My suggestion is that you return to Cuba," looking directly at Costa, "and you, Mr. Fernández, stay here in Nassau to join my security team. Your experience with the G2 could be useful on my staff. I can shield you from General Diego. He has limited authority over Cuba's international affairs."

Fernández did not want to leave Cuba, but he did not want to return to face the general either. It did not take him long to see this was a viable alternative to punishment for again failing to capture Matvey, the thief of the cross and assailant of the art professor.

Realizing the ambassador's offer was his only choice, he replied, "Yes, that is a good plan. I appreciate your kindness."

Costa said, "Yes sir, I am ready to go home. They drive on the wrong side of the street here, and I may get killed in the crosswalks looking the wrong way!"

The ambassador smiled, "Good. It is settled, but there are two things I require you do. First, you must dispose of the casket you procured to hide the prisoner you do not have. And second, you must give up on your efforts to arrest the fugitive. He is a criminal and, as such, is insulting to the Republic. But, he will be a diplomatic nightmare if he is caught. Let God, or Fidel…," pausing, the ambassador looked up toward the ceiling as if he were looking to heaven. Continuing, he said, "…deliver his punishment wherever he goes when he dies."

Costa swallowed hard to accept giving up on the pursuit. Fernández knew he had no other option. With their promise to comply, the ambassador left the room. In a day or two, Fernández would begin a new job and Costa would return to his existing one.

The two men left the ambassador's office. Costa was pleased that he would be home soon, even if it was without the criminal he was after. Fernández had mixed emotions about starting a new life in a strange country and losing his prominent secret police status. He was resigned to accept the only choice he had. He hoped being part of the diplomatic staff would not be a bad job.

Costa promised Fernández that he would figure out a way to get his things to Nassau so he could begin living in The Bahamas. He said to Fernández, "It will be difficult to leave Cuba, my friend. But maybe having a little piece of Cuba with you, here in Nassau, will help with the change. At least you will be able to visit Cuba whenever the ambassador returns to Havana."

Costa asked, "Now what do we do about the casket? It's still in the embassy van. The ambassador wants us to get rid of it."

Fernández replied, "Let's drive around and see if there is a place we can dump it. I don't think we can just leave it on the road. There must be a forest somewhere where we can leave it."

Costa suggested, "Maybe we could take it back to the funeraria?"

"Good idea! Maybe the boss will give back our money."

As they pulled into the funeral home, there was a funeral in progress. Cars were lined up, ready to accompany the hearse to a cemetery. Undeterred, the two men were on a mission and went inside to the parlor.

A receptionist asked, "Gentlemen, are you here for Mrs. Johnson's funeral? If so, you are too late. We are about to drive to the cemetery for her graveside ceremony and interment."

"No, we are here to see the man in charge – the director. I think his name was Pinto or something like that."

"Oh, you must mean Director Pinder," as she emphasized the "der." "May I ask why you want to see him? He is very busy at the moment. Perhaps I can help?"

Costa responded, "We have a casket to return."

Surprised, the receptionist replied, "I'm not sure we accept returns of used caskets. Is it empty?"

"Yes, of course it is! We don't need it anymore. It has not been used. Our friend did not die, so we don't need it," exclaimed Fernández. Costa nodded vigorously in agreement.

"Just a minute. I will get Mr. Pinder." She continued, "But, like I said, we are really busy now. Perhaps you can wait in our lobby."

Costa and Fernández took a seat on a bench near the exit. Well-dressed Bahamians were exiting the sanctuary where Mrs.

Johnson's service had been held and moving through the lobby toward the front doors. For this very formal occasion, the men were dressed in suits. The women were wearing black fancy dresses and flamboyant hats, many with veils that covered their faces. The attendees were in various stages of distress. Many, both men and women, were in tears. A few were overcome with grief, frantically wailing as they were being escorted to the waiting vehicles. A pastor approached Fernández and Costa.

"I'm Reverend Willie Ingraham," introducing himself. "I didn't see you at the funeral." Grabbing their hands to shake, he asked, "How did you know Mrs. Johnson? She was so beloved, and a friend to all. Will you be joining us at the grave site?"

Reverend Ingraham had caught the men off guard and they did not know how to react. They simply blurted out, in unison, "We did not know the dead lady." Fernández concluded by saying, "We are here to return a casket."

Now the reverend was caught off guard, without words. Returning a casket was outside of his experience. "Well, gentlemen, I wish you well and bid you a blessed day!" The preacher scurried out the door to attend to his responsibilities.

Waiting for longer than they had the patience for, the two vexed Cubans started wandering through the funeral home, entering another room set up for visitation. Curious, and, being police officers, not at all distressed by the sight of dead people, they approached an open casket. A younger gentleman, dressed in work clothes, and wearing dark sunglasses, was lying in peaceful repose.

Costa observed, "Looks like this man died young. He is not clothed in a burial suit."

With that, the young man woke up and grabbed the edge of the casket to pull himself up from his nap. His fingers touched Fernández's hand that rested on the edge.

The two tough-guy macho cops bolted from the room and pushed out through the crowd, knocking over flower arrangements in their desperate exit. Running from the entrance back to the embassy van, they opened the rear doors and pushed out their empty casket, leaving it to bounce onto the concrete drive as they sped off. At this point, they were not concerned about getting their money back.

Mrs. Johnson's mourners were momentarily distracted from their grief by the panicked exit of the Cubans. Mr. Pinder observed their speedy retreat and, turning toward Reverend Ingraham, he could only remark, "My apologies. Those are two crazy Cubans."

EIGHTEEN

At the Callaloo Cay Club, Matvey's first assignment was to help the maintenance crew clean and repair gutters at the resort. Water being precious on the island, rainwater was collected in the gutters and channeled to a series of cisterns. The supply of water was used for purposes like laundry or watering the gardens, tasks that did not require potable water. The drinking water was produced by the resort's reverse osmosis desalinization unit.

The facilities supervisor, George Adderley, kept a close eye on Matvey, not expecting this blonde kid to be a capable, hard worker. Matvey was aware he was being watched and evaluated, so he worked extra hard to prove himself in every job he was assigned to. It was natural for him to get along well with everyone at the resort. He respected that everyone was an important part of a successful operation. He wanted to fit in, knowing it was a small island, with a captive, but willing, workforce. Matvey's experience growing up and working in a resort in Cuba taught him that harmony among the workers was important. Here, at this resort, it was especially important. Once on the island, everything a person, whether staff or guests, needed was provided, and it was very hard to leave until the resort provided transportation.

Everything at the resort was designed to meet high standards for the upscale guests. The resort's owners and management staff knew that most of their clientele would expect they would be "roughing it" because the resort was located on a remote island. The goal at Callaloo was to dispel that notion.

In the past, guests might have been roughing it on this remote island. Before the island was redeveloped into Callaloo Cay Club, the property was a small-scale resort for people coming to go fishing for bonefish. It had been a rustic lodge, with a small marina and residences for the owner-operators and a few workers. As the owners aged out, their property was listed for sale.

A consortium of wealthy former clients joined together to purchase the island and redevelop the site into a discreet exclusive resort. The Club's intent was to provide every accommodation and exceed the expectations of its guests. No expense or effort was spared for comfort, privacy, and convenience. A stay at the resort was expected to be no less than a five-star experience, even though it was located on a remote out-island. Little of the former fishing outpost remained as evidence of the long history and loving labors of the original owners.

Matvey worked well with the resort's crew. His upbringing had prepared him for any task whether it was in the kitchen, on the grounds, or in the laundry. With no guests present, he did not need to tap into his customer service personality. At Callaloo there were no lonely ladies to entertain and seduce. He was not tempted into the larceny of his past in Cuba where he danced with the wealthy bejeweled women, getting them to acquiesce to his seductive maneuvers and then taking one piece of their jewelry as an unsentimental memento. The stolen jewelry in Cuba has been an important source of income that he used to supplement his meager wages.

A week passed. Matvey made friends with all of the staff. But, his focus was on the beautiful Puerto Rican, Clara Ruiz.

Housing for the permanent workers was set away from the main campus, but close enough for easy access. It was established to be its own self-sufficient village, enhanced with amenities like a rec room, for the workers' off-hours. In contrast, temporary workers, like Matvey, were assigned small rooms in a building in the maintenance yard, located on an interior site in the coppice forest, well away from the main campus. The small rooms were adequate and nicely appointed. The owners had not skimped on the comfort of the workers, knowing happy workers made for a smooth-running operation.

On the highest point on the cay, a central lodge housed the executive staff in nicely appointed apartments. Mr. Knowles, the manager, as well as the chef, and Clara each had one unit with one unit kept on standby for emergencies. The lodge was the only structure visible to passing boats. It towered above the trees, looking like a contemporary Bahamian mansion.

The resort kitchen was originally designed by a noted chef who set up a variety of menus to complement local Bahamian fare. Adjoining a bar and lounge, the dining room was decorated as an homage to the vintage Bahamian fishing lodges like the one Hemingway frequented on Bimini. A large lobby was available for parties, intimate concerts, or casual lounging. Central to the space was a concert-sized Steinway piano, often played by a performer brought in from a nearby island. Occasionally a guest would be a well-known musician who used the piano to practice or entertain.

The maintenance facility had a shop, barn, greenhouse, and utilities. A backup diesel generator was in a separate structure at the other end of the workyard. An acre of graded hardpan was used for parking vehicles and heavy equipment. Several land-sea metal containers were positioned for storage. The entire compound was surrounded by a four-foot tall stuccoed Bahamian rock wall.

The island hosted an elite clientele of the world's rich and famous. From celebrities to mega-millionaires, Callaloo Cay was an idyllic luxury Caribbean retreat. The architectural vernacular of the bungalows was distinctly authentic Bahamian on the outside, with a few adaptations for porches, verandas, and private mini-pools with solar-heated hot tubs. With eight luxury bungalows, up to 30 guests could be served at the Club. The guest village was laid out so each bungalow had a view of the ocean and was a sufficient distance from other structures to give a sense of privacy.

The inside decor of the guest cottages was modern and clean, with exotic tropical woods and tiled surfaces throughout. Only the exposed common frame ceilings overhead reflected the traditional Bahamian exterior. Everything was designed to create an atmosphere of casual elegance. The Club touted its environmental credentials by claiming to be 100% solar powered and a zero-carbon operation with LEED Platinum buildings.

Workers signed on for year-long contracts and were paid well. The Callaloo Cay Club wisely considered the needs of the workers so, no matter their position within the hierarchy, they would be good at their jobs and happy with their accommodations. Any discord could manifest into something that impacted the guests and the main objective was perfection in every aspect of the resort. Most workers had a long-term relationship with the Club. Any new employees were referred by the consortium of owners and vetted by coworkers and the management team. The limited staff needed to be harmonious and trusting with each other.

Normally, the staff outnumbered the guests. The ratio of workers to guests was about one and a half to one. The team operating the club included the manager, assistant manager, and front-of-the-house staff. There were maintenance workers, a gardener and groundskeepers, housekeepers, a world-class chef, servers, and kitchen help. A registered nurse served as the resort's health professional and nanny when needed. The waterfront and boats were handled by a dockmaster and two bonefishing and reef-diving guides. The resort marina had a small fleet of Albury skiffs and a comfortable service launch.

Every effort was made to keep the guest census at less than eighteen. A crowded island would not fit with the business model for a luxury island retreat. The guests might not realize how challenging providing first-class facilities and amenities were on a remote island, but neither would they care. Their expectations were high and so was the price.

The island had a very short grass airstrip runway, suitable for a small plane, but the main access was by helicopter. An office on New Providence near the private air terminal served the resort's administrative staff, dedicated pilots, and air support crew. A luxury limousine was available to pick up guests at the international terminal of the Pindling Airport if guests arrived in The Bahamas by commercial plane. Since the resort's 'copters were serviced out of the private terminal, guests arriving in Nassau on their private jets only had a short wait for the transfer to the helicopter pad. With dedicated aircraft, including a Bell 429, that could take six, possibly seven, guests could be on the island in under two hours. A larger 'copter, an Airbus H160, could transport up to 12 guests from New Providence in about an hour's flight. The guests certainly did not care that the fossil fuel consumption for the helicopters and supply ships was not factored into the resort's "zero-carbon" claims.

Overall, this resort was exclusive, pricey, and discreet. Membership in the Club was by invitation and cost a $100,000 initiation fee and $24,000 annual dues. This only afforded access and referral privileges. A three-night honeymoon package, subject to availability and approval, would cost newlyweds $25,000 and 22% gratuity to be distributed to the staff with additional tipping optional. Booking the entire resort could cost a wealthy client well over a quarter million dollars for the week. The island would be entirely theirs with access to any amenities. Special activities were available if requested in advance.

Callaloo was acclaimed as tops in facilities, venue, and service. To maintain a superior level of service and ensure a special vacation, even the guests had restrictions, but only two. The first was to avoid the staff village and maintenance area and the second was, of course, to exhibit proper decorum.

Matvey saw some similarities to the Girón resort. Yet, this resort was much more extravagant, more opulent, and more exclusive than anything he had ever seen. There were so few people and so much individual attention.

The people he worked with were all friendly and professional at their jobs. They were kind to him, even as a new person thrown into the mix, and appreciated his help. Even Clara had lightened up after his first week and actually smiled at him on occasion. Matvey was smitten, well on his way to deep infatuation, with her. First, though he needed to secure a permanent position at the Club.

When he was in his second week on the job, two young couples and a family arrived to stay at the Club. Since it was tween-season and a work crew was set to return the following week for extensive remodeling work on several of the bungalows, the Club only accepted a light schedule. Even at such outrageous prices, the Club was in demand, especially during the prime weather season.

The helicopter arrived with the family and one young couple. The family was a middle-aged man and wife with two young teenage daughters. They were from Atlanta. The couple were younger, on their honeymoon, both basking in their wedding's romantic afterglow.

Matvey watched Clara in action. Welcoming the new arrivals, with her uniformed assistant, the ladies were presented with orchid blossoms grown in the on-site greenhouse. Maintenance workers in pressed uniforms handled their luggage while Clara showed the guests to their respective cottages.

An hour later another helicopter arrived to deliver the other couple. They were on a vacation with no special occasion, only seeking peace and quiet. They were dressed in elegant casual attire, ready to see what amenities the resort had to offer. Matvey watched Clara and her assistant repeat the welcome ritual. The woman was indifferent to the flowers she was presented.

For the next few days, Matvey would observe the operation of the resort with just a few guests. He took note of the scheduled meals, leisure activities, and how special requests were handled.

When guests were present, the dress code for staff was different from the down times they had been enjoying. All staff wore uniforms when working. Casual dress was allowed only in the worker housing area and, even then, it had to be presentable, not flip flops and cutoffs.

Every staff member had been trained to be friendly to the clients, but not intrusive. The conduct code required deferential separation of workers from guests. Special requests were given immediate attention, directed to the appropriate staff, and addressed quickly.

Matvey was working at the garden patio, assigned to the groundskeeper for the day. He was tasked with sweeping the sand into a graceful pattern, clearing the sidewalks of leaves and debris, and carefully pruning bougainvillea hedges. The family walked by so Matvey put down his sheers and stepped back away from their path as he had observed other staff do.

When the family passed he saw the two young girls whisper to each other. They turned and squealed, "You look just like one of Ritiki's dancers! Oh my God! It is you! We saw the YouTube video of the Miami concert! Wow! I can't believe it! You caught her fall from the tower!"

Matvey demurred. He liked that he'd been recognized, but he was not happy that he had attracted attention.

The girl's mother chided her daughters, "Girls! Oh, please! Leave this man alone. He works here. Not with that new singer you've been so obsessed with."

"But Mom, it IS him!" Turning to Matvey, they demanded, "Tell her – it's you."

Matvey just smiled. Hearing the commotion, Clara came to intervene.

Clara said, "Can I be of assistance?"

The mother said, "My daughters think this man is a dancer who performed at a concert with a pop singer."

"Mom, it's him!"

154

Clara offered, "I'm sure it's just mistaken identity. This is Matvey, a new, temporary, addition to our staff." Looking at him, she said, "He's a temporary worker at Callaloo Cay Club," reemphasizing the word temporary. She glared at Matvey, assuming that he was making a scene and violating the Club's strict rules.

Clara asked, "Matvey, would you tell them, were you a dancer or not?"

Matvey looked down, a little embarrassed. "Yes, I was on tour with Ritiki Boca de Caroni. She is so nice and very talented. But now I am here." Looking directly into Clara's eyes, he added, "And I hope I can stay!"

"See, I knew it! He's been close to Ritiki! I just LOVE her! Mom? Dad? Can we ask Matvey to give us a dance lesson?"

The father put down the request, "I'm sure that's not part of his job. You will just have to watch the videos and we will look for a dance studio when we get back to Atlanta."

Clara knew the rule: All reasonable and legal guest requests would be honored to create special memories. "I am sure we can arrange something for these wonderful young ladies, that is if Matvey is agreeable."

Matvey smiled, "Yes, of course." He wanted to get back in Clara's good graces. He knew the rule about special requests, too.

Clara asked, "When would you like to schedule a lesson?"

The girls shrieked, in a pitch that could almost shatter glass. "Any time! We love Ritiki! She's so beautiful! And this man knows her! He danced with her, and he can dance with us!" Although they knew it was not lady-like decorum, they jumped up and down with enthusiasm. Their parents were pleased their daughters would be engaged with something real instead of their incessant occupation with the Internet.

Clara suggested, "How about in a couple hours, after you return from exploring the beach?"

An hour later, Matvey was wearing a customer service uniform of a pastel batik camp shirt and tan pants. He had his mobile phone cued to play several different songs that he Bluetoothed to the lounge sound system.

While Clara waited in the lounge with Matvey, she cleared the dance floor and instructed him on the resort's protocol. Only the bartender, Miss Ceilly, and the honeymoon couple were in the lounge at the time. The couple were sitting at the bar, obsessed with each other over tall fruity drinks.

The girls raced in, dressed in their casual sundresses and low-heeled sandals. As they stood before Matvey, they exclaimed excitedly, "We are ready! We want to dance like Ritiki!"

Matvey instructed, "First we will see how you dance. You should dance with each other to do the salsa." To the taller girl, he asked, "What is your name? You should be the lead."

She was thrilled. "I am Morgan. This is my sister, Hannah."

"My name is Matvey. Nice to meet you both. Well, Morgan, you take the hand of Hannah and show me your salsa!" Matvey pushed the play button on his iPhone.

The girls performed OK, especially for young people new to the dance. As Matvey coached them, they improved.

"Now, let's try some of Ritiki's music!" First, Matvey performed the dance steps solo. Then he took Morgan's hand to slowly work through the moves with her. She was over the moon. "Now, your sister, Hannah!"

Hannah was a little less capable but still doing her best. She was overjoyed and worked hard to please Matvey.

Then, the girls demanded, "Show us how you dance - maybe with the lady." They were pointing to Clara, who shook her head vigorously, no!

Matvey whispered in Clara's ear "All guests requests, reasonable and legal…" Clara frowned but agreed.

Matvey played a well-known salsa song on his phone. Clara was no professional, but salsa was in her Puerto Rican DNA. She did well, and to the people in the lounge, Clara and Matvey dancing together was as compelling a dance as they had ever seen. The honeymoon couple came from the bar with their drinks to watch. The girls stood at the edge of the dance floor with their parents behind them. Everyone was swaying with the music. To finish the dance, Matvey spun Clara, lowering her to his knee, and looking into her eyes. Now he could tell she was smitten with him.

After a few more lessons on Ritiki's signature dance moves and teaching everyone in the bar, including Miss Ceilly the bartender, the Bollywood line dance, the lesson ended. Everyone clapped. Here was an intimate audience, not the 80,000 at Hard Rock Stadium, but they were just as appreciative.

As the parents walked out, they thanked Matvey and pulled Clara aside. The gentleman said, "I've just joined the board of the Club corporation. We are here to connect with our girls while I get familiar with your operation. I hope you will keep Matvey on your staff. He seems to be a real asset."

Clara thought so too, but would not admit it, to him or to herself.

The next day, Matvey's contract was extended for six months. He moved to the permanent worker village.

NINETEEN

Matvey's absence in Nassau had been noticed by his friends, both the ones at the cafe and those who were with him on tour. His disappearance was very concerning. Nigel and Hector were more worried than usual because they speculated that the two Cuban "friends" were cops and that they could have taken Matvey. In addition to those two, Ritiki Boca de Caroni's manager asked Nigel and Hector if they had seen or heard from Matvey, knowing that they were all friends.

They began to think that maybe he wasn't in Miami like he said he would be. They reasoned he would have come back to Nassau at some point to collect his things. Now, everything he owned was being hauled out of his apartment. He was being evicted for not paying the rent for months. Their attempts to contact him were unsuccessful. Emails were returned. They had his cell number but when they called they could never reach him. His Bahamas phone account rang through as "no longer in service."

Months passed since Matvey had been given a contract to join the Callaloo Club's permanent staff. He had proven to be a valuable addition. He became the administrative assistant to the general manager, learning how to address every detail of the resort's operations. His affable personality endeared him to guests and his willingness to get his hands dirty was respected by his coworkers.

Realizing that they were on a remote island, the Club would arrange short off-island visits to let the staff have some free time to conduct affairs and stretch their legs in a larger community on another island. On one of these trips to George Town, Exuma, Matvey reinstated his BTC Bahamas phone account and he transferred his Barclays Bank account from Nassau to the local branch.

Once the phone was again active, Matvey could see that he had many emails. He couldn't get the voicemails left on the phone, but he could retrieve the emails. He saw all of them stacked up, from Nigel, Mr. Roque, Mr. Cross, and Cali, as well as a clutter of spam. He couldn't bring himself to read them right then. He didn't want to be reminded of the past, of having to abandon his life as a dancer with Ritiki, and the friends he had made in Nassau. He needed to focus on his new life, but the emails haunted him.

On one of his days off, Matvey hitched a ride on the resort's launch to nearby Cat Island. He needed time to himself to think things through. After being dropped off, he sat on a bench by the sea on the dock at the Bight settlement on Cat Island. Here, alone, he read the emails. The messages in the emails became increasingly more urgent as they got closer to the present day. Several advised him of the eminent eviction from his apartment. Strangely enough, he had never given his place in Nassau another thought since he arrived at Callaloo Cay. This place felt like home. It was where he wanted to be. But, he missed his friends from the cafe, and Hector and Nigel.

Matvey thought about what he should do to answer the emails. "Nobody knows where I am and that is good for me. If my friends don't know where I am then the Cubans can't find me here." But he was concerned that his friends were worried about him.

Mr. Roque and Mr. Cross wanted to sign him up for another tour. "What should I tell them? I really enjoyed being on tour. I went so many places and I got to dance with the best." While thinking about his past, Matvey realized that he wanted the simpler life of the Callaloo Cay Club. He would have to decide, but maybe not now. Memories of the past, both bad and good, and thoughts of his future were overwhelming. It was easier to defer making any decisions.

Walking along the road, he noticed a sign at an intersection by a small store. The sign pointed to a place called "The Hermitage." He went inside the store to buy a bottle of water.

Matvey asked the clerk, "Can you explain the sign to me?"

The heavy-set lady sitting at a counter behind a clutter of merchandise look puzzled. Matvey pointed outside toward the street corner with the sign and clarified his question, "The sign that shows the way to her-mit-age."

"Oh, that," she replied, "It's the place Father Jerome, a Catholic priest, built for himself to retire to in about 1939. It's on the highest point in all of The Bahamas, up that mountain - Mount Alvernia. It's really not a mountain. It's a hill a couple hundred feet high, but we like to say mountain. The Catholic Church is in charge of the place. You should go see! The view is lovely."

Matvey thanked her, saying as he started to walk out of the store, "Maybe I will walk up."

The clerk was not done telling him. "You can walk the Stations of the Cross. There's a steep path that the old monk created so he could do his daily devotions. The place at the top is all his stonework. Father Jerome built a lot of churches – around the world, actually. He's really famous."

Matvey had heard more than he needed. He said "Thank you. Muchas gracias, señora," hoping speaking Spanish might give him an exit from the exuberant lecture. He started up the road to the site. On the way he saw a sign with an arrow, "Mount Alvernia." This name sounded close to Alvero. He wiped the sweat from his brow and continued walking, recounting his encounter on the boat and escaping Alvero's filet knife.

Talking to himself and the wind and the sun, he said aloud, "I am so lucky. I got out of Cuba. I survived the hurricane. I found new friends. I danced with a star in shows around the Caribbean and now I am at the place I want to be. I only have to win Clara and my life will be good." He reflected on how his relationship with Clara had blossomed. He was moving toward a marriage proposal. "I will wait until I know she can't say no."

Reaching the top of the hill, he saw the structures the monk had built. It was amazing that an old man did the work all by himself, lifting and moving stones into place to create a chapel, a well, and small place for him to eat, sleep, and reflect.

Looking out at the horizon there was a 360-degree view of the island, the Atlantic, Exuma Sound, and both the north and south end of Cat Island fading into the humid haze. The coppice forest carpeted the lands below him. A Bahamas mockingbird serenaded him with a song.

Matvey was awestruck. Thinking out loud, he shouted to no one in particular. "This is so beautiful!" Realizing he was in a sacred space, he lowered his voice as he vowed, "Someday I will share this place with Clara. This is the place where I will ask her to marry me. If she says no, I'll jump off the cliff." Then he laughed.

His mood sank while he reminisced about his recent turbulent past. He sat on the bench inside the small stone chapel that Father Jerome had crafted. Light streamed through a circular window above the modest altar. Matvey was not spiritual and had no upbringing in the Catholic Church. Cuba's official state religion was secular communism. But, sitting in this place, he felt an inner peace. The setting moved him to reflect more about his life.

"I was happy in Cuba in Girón. I did not know about the rest of the world, except what I could see on the Internet, when we could get it." He kicked the ground at his feet. "I was okay. Then everything happened so fast."

Many thoughts raced through his mind. Meeting Evelyn at the Girón resort, having to run away in the boat, wrecking on the island, Sunny . . . "All I have been doing is drifting with the tide. I didn't have a plan. Even my dancing with Ritiki was adjusting to an opportunity. It wasn't a plan. Now, I have a plan. This is what I want."

In this place of peace and solitude, the future he wanted became clear. He resolved, "I will stay at Callaloo with Clara! I will make this happen and not just be moved by the current."

It was time for him to return to the dock. The shore excursion was over and the boat would take him back to Callaloo Cay. He was anxious to resume his duties and his courtship of Clara. He told himself, "From now on, I'm acting, not reacting."

Stopping again at the store, he wanted to buy a suitable gift for Clara. Noticing there wasn't much to choose from, Matvey settled on a faded silk rose, embossed with "A Souvenir of Cat Island."

As he boarded the Club launch to return to Callaloo Cay, he knew that he would not answer the emails, at least not right away. He would not return to tour with Ritiki. That would be as dangerous as it had been a few months ago. But, someday in the future, he would let his friends, Nigel and Hector, and Carmen, Cali, and Carlos, know that he was alive and doing well.

TWENTY

When the Club tender returned Matvey to the island, the staff was abuzz. They had been notified that a megayacht would be arriving and the entire island was reserved for just one client, the owner of the yacht. A few existing bookings had to be canceled, but the anonymous oligarch who had reserved the island for a week offered to pay for any bookings that had to be canceled to fulfill his reservation. The representative of the wealthy person said that many of his own team would be there to assume the duties of the resort's staff, and they would need accommodations on the island if available. Existing resort staff that were not essential would be given a paid vacation off island.

It was clear to Mr. Knowles and Clara that this man, whoever he was, wanted privacy. The agent for the superyacht said, "The captain will be calling you to get local information on where he can anchor and the facilities you have for disembarking passengers from his tender. His yacht is 280 ft. He has several tenders and a small helicopter if you have a landing space."

"Oh yes. In addition to our helipad, we have a small grass landing strip, that we use to bring in guests. Our dockmaster can advise on a place to anchor," Mr. Knowles responded.

The agent was very gracious and professional in asking for details about the property and the facilities they had available. "We will also have our advance security team sweep your property and secure a perimeter. Our employer is very cautious and he personally selected your site for a week so he could relax and have an important meeting. The person he will be meeting will be flying in from Nassau after we make arrangements."

In the past, megayachts had come for several days, not staying their entire minimum five-day reservation. The boats were large enough to be cruise ships, but only carried maybe a dozen guests. Passengers would disembark to enjoy the resort's ample amenities and then move on. Guests were given every attention they wanted or reclusive solitude if that was their preference. Most often they did not require the entire island, so a few other guests could be accommodated as well.

Rarely had the entire Club been reserved by one guest. There had been private weddings and group functions that reserved the entire island for social events or high-profile retreats. But a single guest was unusual. The extreme focus on security was unprecedented and a little disconcerting.

Clara and Mr. Knowles met to discuss logistics. They could assign a couple of bungalows for the staff from the yacht and some workers would be given holiday, while others could stay in reserve to back up whatever the secret guest might need. Up to 10 guests from the yacht could be assigned to six cottages. The yacht's security team could use the temporary worker housing. It was not even certain if the man would be staying on property and not on his ship. All they were told was that he wanted the location for his private meeting.

Meeting with all of the staff, Clara relayed the plan for the upcoming visitor. Their normal operation was serving the wealthy. Now this event would be serving someone who was super wealthy. They wondered who, but only the manager was privileged to know the identity. Mr. Knowles would not disclose it to anyone, not even Clara. "It's best you do not know," he said when she asked. The club's staff took to calling the mysterious guest "Mr. X." The reservation payment, along with an added fee of another $100,000 reserve, for security and incidentals, was made and cleared well in advance of the guest's arrival.

With just a week's notice, the resort staff scrambled to be ready, turn the property into a showcase, and fly in provisions that the yacht owner's team had requested.

On the appointed day, the megayacht arrived, communicating with the dockmaster to coordinate anchoring well off the island in the deeper water. The draft of this boat exceeded the safe anchorage that was suitable for most yachts. It had more crew than the resort's entire staff to attend to the needs of just one owner. Callaloo staff walked to the shore to gawk at the boat that looked like a cruise ship and was so much larger than any vessel they had ever hosted.

A military-looking tender arrived with a uniformed security team. The contingent looked like a special forces group. They had a private conversation with Mr. Knowles and then spread out to secure the perimeter of the island. They had four hours to complete their task. Two men went into the buildings with some kind of electronic equipment, looking for listening devices. Clara showed them the lodge and the guest bungalows. When they returned to the central yard, they radioed the ship that the island was acceptable.

The intrusion of the megayacht's paramilitary security seemed excessive. The armed contingent added even more mystery about the guest. George Adderley and the dockmaster, Grady Greene, were Callaloo's resident security. Usually, their duties involved dissuading unwanted boats from landing at the resort's dock. But, in this special case, their duties were overshadowed by the yacht's team.

A couple of hours later, after the security team was given use of the resort's golf carts and shown to the guest worker housing, men were positioned at the ends of the island. Several were stationed around the putting green-like grassy lawn.

Finally, a fancy tender arrived at the dock. The resort crew assisted with securing the glistening mahogany-trimmed craft. A special ramp was extended for an elderly gentleman who walked with a cane, dressed in a white sport coat, pink pants, and teal silk t-shirt, wearing a fedora. Behind him followed a much younger, slim, tall, shapely, blonde woman, elegantly dressed in a gauzy sundress under a broad-brimmed hat with a silk veil. A dockhand extended a hand to assist her. Then, two couples disembarked from the tender and followed them along the ramp to the dock.

The senior resort employees formed a receiving line to greet and welcome the new arrivals. For each of the female guests, Matvey had a bouquet that had been brought from Nassau with the rest of the provisions.

Mr. Knowles shook hands with the senior patriarch as he gestured to Matvey to present a bouquet to the younger woman who was holding onto the patriarch's arm. She lifted her veil. Matvey's eyes met hers. It was Evelyn! – the English art professor who was the start of his troubles.

Their eyes met and locked for a moment. Each was frozen in a conundrum of how to react. Matvey had a new life at the resort and had put his past behind him. Nobody knew his story and he felt safe, out of the reach of the Cubans. His brief liaison with her was the beginning of the cascade of events that brought him to where he was now.

Evelyn too was in a new place, as the trophy wife of an oligarch. Her days of academia, touring students in Cuba, and art trafficking were left behind when she was taken to be a wealthy man's fancy. She was now above and beyond the reach of those in the ordinary world.

Facing each other, with the memory of a brief tryst they shared, they each realized there was no point in revisiting a past that they left behind and that could not be changed. Outing the history could only jeopardize the future. Matvey looked into Evelyn's eyes to send an apology that he could not verbalize.

Evelyn broke the awkward silence, "Thank you, sir. These are lovely. I'm certain we will have a delightful holiday here on your island."

Evelyn returned a knowing look and then turned away, gently touching the small scar on her forehead, before straightening her hat and calling to her new husband. "Darling, do you think we might have some music and dancing tonight?" she asked as she raced off, taking her husband's arm again.

Neither Matvey nor Evelyn had acknowledged their past.

The couples walked to waiting golf carts for a tour of the Club and to be escorted to their bungalows by Clara and Mr. Knowles.

Matvey was relieved that he survived the improbable encounter with Evelyn and that he had not been assigned to take them to a bungalow. He thought he should make himself as scarce as his responsibilities would allow. He couldn't believe that the part of his past that seemed like a lifetime ago was here in the same place as he. "What are the chances?" he said aloud, as he looked up toward the sun.

Clara returned to the lodge after the three couples settled into their quarters. Each bungalow had an attendant from the ship to take care of the guests. The Club had provisioned the cottages unnecessarily because the yacht crew brought their own supplies that fit the preferences of the guests. A security guard was posted at each villa.

Clara looked at Matvey, "For a moment, it looked like you knew the blonde lady that was with the old man."

Matvey said, "No. I just wanted to see what a rich man's lady looked like. Not my type. I'm in love with a Puerto Rican girl!" he said, breaking into a wide smile in an effort to hide his acquaintance with Evelyn.

Clara confided, "This whole event is weird. Armed guards? Yacht staff replacing our workers. Even the yacht cook took over our kitchen from Chef! It might be a good profit for the Club, but I'll be happy when this is over!"

Clara had arranged for a performer to be singing on the patio after the evening meal. The request for dancing could be fulfilled if that was the guests' pleasure. The local artist, singing Bahamas folk tunes and popular calypso songs, was not high energy. As it turned out, the guests sat outside, away from the solo Bahamian singer, to smoke cigars and have an aperitif. It was a good try but fell short of engaging the guests.

All of the guests retreated to their bungalows about an hour after sunset. The older gentleman stayed behind to tell the manager that his guest would be arriving tomorrow mid-morning for lunch. "My guest and I will need complete privacy." The foreign tycoon was more friendly than expected and graciously thanked Mr. Knowles for the use of the facilities and the hospitality. "I appreciate you arranging entertainment tonight, but please it is not necessary again." The oligarch's accented speech telegraphed he was Russian or Eastern European.

The Club staff performed some cleaning and rearrangement of the lodge and patio. An hour later all were ready for bed. Curious about the mysterious tycoon and anxious about how the rest of his stay would go, they all retired to their quarters. Matvey and Clara hugged before heading to their respective apartments.

TWENTY-ONE

Breakfast the next morning was unremarkable. The yacht chef had prepared a simple meal in the resort's kitchen. After dining, the men met at a table in a gazebo. The ladies went for a walk, asking for someone to guide them on the island trail. A security guard accompanied them while another remained with the men. The men in the security detail looked serious and focused.

It was mid-morning when all of the men in the megayacht party gathered again at the lodge to wait for their guest. The oligarch asked Mr. Knowles and Clara to escort the people who would be arriving to the lodge lounge. Matvey was assigned to collect them by golf cart.

A helicopter flew an approach pattern and then circled the landing pad. The oligarch's security team was at the ready. Mr. Knowles was told that the person the oligarch was meeting with was arriving by private charter. He assumed this was the charter, but he did not know for sure.

The 'copter landed, dusting the waiting security team with a cloud of sand. An additional two security men were hidden in the nearby vegetation with assault rifles. This reminded Matvey of Cuban security when important people met for parties at the Girón resort.

The door opened and two men emerged from the aircraft. They helped a heavy-set middle-aged woman exit the steps. Matvey watched from a safe distance until the security team vetted the helicopter passengers. They were not patted down for firearms but were questioned and even requested to show the team leader their passports. The pilot was powering down the engine and the rotor blades slowed to a stop.

The oligarch's lead security guard led them to where Matvey was standing, in the shade under an arched gate of flowering bougainvilleas. One man followed close behind the guard. Then, 10 meters behind him followed the Cuban ambassador with the woman on his arm. Matvey recognized the Cuban ambassador and hoped the ambassador would not recognize him.

Matvey realized the woman accompanying the ambassador was one of the Castro family. He didn't know how she was related because he knew little of Cuba's politics or who the face cards of the regime were, but he figured she must be estranged from the family. Then again maybe she wasn't. What he was sure of was he had a job to do, and he needed to do it well to make a good impression of the Club on these wealthy and important guests.

When the oligarch's security guard stepped aside for the arriving party to be greeted, Matvey was face to face with his nemesis, Agent Oscar Fernández. Both froze. Time was suspended in an instant of shock. Fernández had to subdue an internal rage, aware that he was in a new position, and had agreed to give up on pursuing Matvey. Matvey had to suppress his fear of this man and the potential for capture by him. He thought again, "What are the chances? My past is haunting me!"

There was a moment of awkward silence when Fernández extended his hand. "You may remember me!" He moved close to Matvey's face. Almost in a whisper, he said, "I was with the G2. I know you are a despicable criminal who should be punished in Cuba for your crimes. But, now I work for the Cuban ambassador to The Bahamas. I'm in a new position. You are no longer my concern. I told you once before and it is still the same. I said on Alvero's boat and I say it again, now in my new job. ¡Me importa tres cojones! You are not anything special! I don't care! It seems we are both in a new life."

The arrival of the ambassador and the lady who were following behind Fernández interrupted the brief confrontation. If the ambassador had recognized Matvey, he didn't acknowledge it. Matvey took them by golf cart to their meeting with the oligarch. He was shaken, yet immensely relieved that Fernández had not arrested him.

With the men and lady in a meeting at the lodge, he had time to return to his apartment. He was greatly disturbed by this chance encounter and the circumstances involved. He desperately wanted to move on with a new life. Now his location was no longer a secret. Fernández may not feel the need to arrest him, but he would surely tell The General, or the captain, Alvero, or even his cohort Costa. Matvey knew he was not safe – again.

While Matvey was in his quarters he retrieved the Crown Royal sack containing the treasures he had managed to hang onto through all of his ordeals. He walked down to the shore and emptied his embroidered royal blue bag of jewels into the lapping waves. Glimmering facets of rubies, amethysts, diamonds, and pearls twinkled in the sunlight before descending into the sand and shells. Each jewel was a memento of his theft of a vulnerable lady's heart.

Looking to the horizon, toward Cuba, he said out loud, "I am rich enough here. I want nothing of my past. I want only my future and it is here. Adios Cuba, mi amor." Superstitiously, he hoped discarding the jewelry, representing the beginnings of his old life, would bring him luck in a new life. He said goodbye to his homeland, purging his conscience of his thievery and vowing to start fresh.

Clara had followed him down the path. "Hey, Matvey! What are you doing?" Not waiting for an answer she exclaimed, "Good news! They are done. The rich old man and the trophy consort on his arm are leaving soon. The ambassador and his party already departed."

She was happy. "I overheard them say 'We will meet again soon. Next time in Cuba.' I wonder what they are planning?"

He thought to himself, "Now, it is my turn to say ¡Me importa tres cojones! I don't give a damn!"

Matvey smiled and said to Clara, "Good! This will be our paradise island again. My place is here with you." He fervently hoped it would be so, with no more interference from his past. He was keenly aware that his secret depended on the discretion of Evelyn and Fernández.

TWENTY-TWO

The Callaloo Cay Resort returned to the normal activity of hosting privacy-seeking, well-off guests, not that the operation was ever routine, with catering to the needs and whims of privileged patrons and the challenges of maintaining five-star standards on a remote island outpost. The arrival of club members was a welcome change after hosting the oligarch who took over the resort.

Mr. Knowles called Matvey to his office. Expecting a special assignment, Matvey was surprised to learn that Mr. Knowles had been contacted by Mr. Roque, Ritiki's manager, and had scheduled a brief visit along with the arrival of guests on the next helicopter.

"What can he want?"

Mr. Knowles answered, "He wants to talk with you about joining the singer Ritiki for a performance in the Cayman Islands. He said he would need you for a week. Frankly, I'm a little amazed at this. I didn't know much about your past, other than you had been in some kind of show before coming here."

Matvey was confused. "I don't know how he found me. I've been out of touch with the Ritiki company since coming here. This is my new life and that is in the past. I am sorry for this."

"You don't need to apologize. We'd hate to lose you, but don't want to stand in your way... that is if you want to do something else."

"NO! No, my life is here with Clara. I am very happy to be here, to do whatever you need from me. No, I don't want to talk to him. Please tell him not to come!"

"I'm afraid it's a little too late for that. He's on the helicopter that's on its way now and they'll be here in an hour."

Matvey was upset to have this part of his past catch up with him and complicate his life and maybe even jeopardize his job. Once again, he was reacting to circumstances, rather than creating opportunities.

"I am so sorry Mr. Knowles. I did not want the managers of Ritiki's tour to contact me. I did not tell them I was here."

TWENTY-THREE

Matvey anxiously waited for the helicopter to land. As soon as he completed his task to meet the new arrivals he would speak with Mr. Roque. He wanted to get this over with and sever his ties with Ritiki. He was very worried that Mr. Knowles would lose confidence in him.

Mr. Roque was waiting in the main lounge of the lodge. Matvey rushed to meet him, extending his hand and immediately saying, "No, Mr. Roque, I am not available to go back on tour with the company. I am working here now. This is where I want to live."

Roque replied, "Wait, wait, Matvey. I'm glad to see you, let me explain first. It took us some time to track you down. Don't blame Nigel, but when you let him know you were OK and not coming back to Nassau, we contacted the bank where we deposited your checks. They told us you moved your account to George Town, Exuma. Then we visited and spoke to people there to finally find you here at this resort. It looks like a pretty nice place."

"Yes, it is, and I am happy here. Sorry that I did not let you know." Matvey was chagrined that he should have let them know he had left Nassau and would not be coming back.

"Well, the reason I am here is that we need you to help Ritiki with a showcase program she is doing for some big London entertainment producers. They are considering putting her under contract. She's got a demo set up in the Cayman Islands for them in a couple of weeks. She's not going to perform with the whole troupe, just a short program with only the band, backup singers, and three dancers. She really wants you to do the salsa routine. Nigel and Hector are set."

"I'm sorry, I have my job here. I can't..."

Roque snapped, "Yes, you can! I already cleared it with Mr. Knowles. When I explained how much we did for you to get you a passport and work permit, he thought it would only be right for you to do this one-time favor in return."

"Please, a moment. I know you did much to help me. I am truly grateful. Let me think and speak with Clara."

"OK, but don't take too long. I have to return to Nassau on the helicopter. I'm not leaving with a 'no.'"

Matvey spoke with Clara and Mr. Knowles. They agreed he should do this for his former employers, but hoped he would return to Callaloo Cay Resort. He returned to the lounge to tell Mr. Roque, "I will go, but just this once, for Ritiki and only if I can I bring Clara along."

"Great. I knew I could count on you. I'll arrange a seat for Clara. We have chartered a jet. There will be a few days of rehearsals in Nassau before we leave for Cayman. We'll only be in Grand Cayman for three nights. Then you can get back to your life here in a week and we won't bother you again. Of course, unless you want us to," Roque grinned. "I've got to get back and prep. See you next week in Nassau! We will arrange your transportation." Matvey asserted, "And Clara too!" Then Roque was off on the resort's transport back to Nassau.

Matvey and Clara discussed the plan with Mr. Knowles. "You can go, for a week. But only for a week. I can't lose both of you - I can't lose either of you! If you don't come back, I guess it won't matter if I fire you!"

TWENTY-FOUR

The oligarch's giant yacht departed Callaloo for a rendezvous in Sint Maarten. Along with the oligarch Nicholai Klotchkof's ship, several other megayachts met there each year off Philipsburg. Only a few crew came ashore for a re-supply of fresh stores. Few people in the town knew who was on the yachts, or what they were doing. They only knew it was a regular annual occurrence. From the hills overlooking Simpson Bay, observers could see the tenders scurry back and forth between the yachts. Curious residents wondered if the meet-up of these obviously privileged individuals was simply social or business, or perhaps something more sinister. What everyone knew was the wealth of the owners put them in an elite class, separate from ordinary people and mostly out of the reach of governments.

Sightseers and private boats that came close to the megayachts were escorted away. Each cruise ship-sized boat had a well-armed security force aboard to deter unwanted guests or repel pirate attacks. While anchored in the bay, protection was provided by the Dutch Caribbean Coast Guard, allowing the on-board security to stand watch on the vessel.

Russian oligarchs, like Klotchkof, had prospered by leveraging the assets they skimmed during the dissolution of the Soviet Union. Their financial interests were secure so long as their operations were aligned with Moscow politics. One major concern now was a growing trend of Western nations imposing sanctions and limiting trade. Fewer countries were welcoming their megayachts, hampering travel and their annual rendezvous. Some nations had even threatened to confiscate their ships to settle debts of the Russian government.

The growing antipathy of foreign nations to the oligarchs resulted in reducing the places they could visit. Increased scrutiny of who was invited to their offshore gatherings called for more privacy. The consensus among the Russians was that Cuba might be a more friendly and discreet location for their aggregations as well as an exotic venue for on-shore exploration. The next stop for Klotchkof would be the island nation for a meeting with authorities to explore establishing a friendly, secure destination for future meet-ups.

Nicolai Klotchkof had sent his personnel ahead of his arrival in Cuba to assess a location that might be suitable for developing as a private harbor retreat. His assistant developed several proposals for presentation to the oligarch's peers. Though he could easily fund the development of a safe harbor venue, it was his objective to have several partners share in the venture.

When all of his associates were gathered in the large, opulently-decorated main saloon of his megayacht, Klotchkof spoke. "Gentlemen I need your investment; your partnership. You know our world is shrinking. You are all aware how suitable venues for us are now limited and getting even more scarce. Nothing exists for us unless we create a place for ourselves, a location where we can be private and safe. By all accounts, Cuba is a friendly place. With Miss Castro's assistance, and the help of the Cuban ambassador to The Bahamas, we can make a haven for all of us there. I have recently met with these people to explore new possibilities."

The presentation of the idea of a private port located on the southern coast of Cuba continued.

"With a deep port, convenient airport, and suitably-sized clean urban center, Cienfuegos is the leading contender. The Bay of Pigs is also a possibility if Fidel's venerated so-called 'secret' waterfront installation can be negotiated for purchase. The military presence there presents positive benefits as well as a political obstacle, but not an insurmountable challenge for any or all of us. Let us work together to make Cuba our next ultimate, private place to gather."

The wealthy group of oligarchs embraced the idea in concept. Several were enthusiastic and anxious to be partners in the venture. The general opinion was for the idea to continue on the progress that had already been made with the Cuban ambassador to The Bahamas and the Castro heir. They resolved to meet in Cienfuegos for a trial run of the harbor and personal survey of potential sites. Klotchkof agreed to continue his efforts to gain the approval of the Cuban regime.

TWENTY-FIVE

It was time for Matvey to travel to Nassau for the rehearsals. Clara would join him in a couple of days to make the charter flight from Nassau to Grand Cayman. Leaving was tearful even though their absence would be short. It was the first time they would be apart since they had become a devoted couple. Matvey boarded the resort's transport helicopter and took off to Nassau.

Rehearsals went well. Matvey had not lost much in his step. The practices he had before the big tour of the Caribbean prepped him with muscle memory of the choreography. Ritiki was pleased to have her proficient partner back with her. She had a lot riding on this performance for the London corporate media moguls.

The abbreviated show would include Matvey's salsa dance with Ritiki, a solo song, and an abbreviated Bollywood dance number with Nigel and Hector, concluding with a high-powered vocal performance with two backup singers. The show did not need a lot of practice because it was adapted from the Caribbean tour set, but the shortened times of the numbers meant the dance routines needed to be adjusted. As usual, Ritiki's high standards demanded perfection.

Both Roque and Cross were well prepared to show the British media conglomerate the enormous potential of the world market for their client. Roque produced a short video showing highlights of the Caribbean tour and a compelling summary of the financial metrics and press reactions.

Together, the managers met with the performance team. They reviewed the itinerary and emphasized the importance of this chance for broad international celebrity. Costumes, equipment, and travel plans were checked and double-checked. The passport problems Matvey had before the last tour remained a sensitive concern. Both Mr. Cross and Mr. Roque brought it up during the briefings.

After three days in Nassau, they were ready. Before leaving for the Caymans, the troupe had a light day of rest. Clara joined Matvey in Nassau in an emotional reunion that belied that they had only been separated for a few days.

Matvey introduced Clara to Ritiki. While still at Callaloo, Clara had researched the singer on the Internet and was between starstruck and jealous when meeting this tall, beautiful diva. Matvey was hers; she tightly gripped his hand and hugged his waist as if to claim him as her property. Ritiki was gracious, and complimentary, and thanked her for loaning her man to participate in this demonstration. "Clara, I am indebted to you and so glad you can join this event. Trust me, I will return Matvey to you so you may dance together for the rest of your lives." Ritiki gave them both a disarming smile as she departed. Clara eased her grip on Matvey, a little comforted that this charismatic lady was not her rival.

Ritiki's advance team in Cayman had reported that all arrangements were in place and the venue would be ready. The troupe was scheduled to arrive in Cayman a couple of days before the presentation. With dress rehearsals scheduled before the arrival of the Brits, they would have time to make any last-minute adjustments before the audition event.

The charter jet was loaded and ready to take off. Excitement swirled through the plane's cabin as the engines roared and they sped down the runway. Everyone applauded when they lifted off and banked to the west. Matvey pointed out to Clara Clifton Bay and the development where Ritiki lived. Clara strained to see what he was trying to show her, but she only noticed the beautiful light aqua and deep blue waters and the olive green woodlands of the New Providence landscape. Climbing higher to cruising altitude, the Captain announced the flight plan would be one hour fifty-three minutes, cruising at 25,000 feet. "Welcome aboard, this flight is from Nassau to George Town, Grand Cayman." He continued by reporting on the weather in the Caymans and that the flight would take them over central Cuba, before descending to land in George Town.

Flying over a low ceiling of clouds, they caught brief glimpses of the ocean below. Both Matvey and Clara hoped they could see Callaloo out the left side of the plane, but clouds obscured their view as they passed over the island.

Matvey assured Clara that they would be back to normal after this excursion. "Thank you for allowing me to do this. I owe a lot to these people who helped me get legal in The Bahamas. If they had not worked out my passport and immigration problems, I would have never met you."

Clara just smiled and squeezed his hand.

About 45 minutes into the flight the captain came on the loudspeaker. "Ladies and gentlemen, we have a small problem with our aircraft. There's an indicator light that shows we have an issue with our hydraulic pressure. Just to be safe, we're going to land in Cuba to have this problem checked out. It may be nothing, but we'd like you to return to your seats and fasten your seatbelts. Flight attendants, please prepare the cabin."

The flight attendants quickly passed through the cabin, collecting materials and directing everyone to buckle their seatbelts and move their seat backs to an upright position. The captain's announcement and attendant activity had everyone's attention. Nobody was panicked but all were looking around for answers that none of them had.

The Captain made another announcement, "Passengers, we have clearance to land in Cienfuegos, Cuba where we can get our aircraft checked out and repaired if necessary. I'm sure there is no problem. Please stay calm and we will be safely on the ground in a few minutes." He tried to lighten up the tension by saying "There will be no extra charge for visiting Cuba on our trip."

Looking out the window they could see a Cuban jet fighter on the wing, escorting the plane to Cienfuegos. This added to the anxiety of engine trouble and the unscheduled landing. The fighter stayed with the plane all the way to the airport, matching its speed and course. Matvey wondered if there was a problem beyond the mechanical failure. Clara asked Matvey, "Are we being forced to land?" although she knew he couldn't answer her question.

As they touched down and rolled to a stop, everyone applauded. Nervous laughter filled the cabin. As the plane taxied to the terminal, the captain made an announcement.

"Please stay on the plane while the mechanics check out our systems. We hope this will be brief and we can get on our way to George Town."

A few minutes later, the speaker crackled with an update. "The mechanics will need more time to make repairs, so, it looks like you will be visiting Cuba."

When a ground crew rolled stairs up to the side of the plane, and the cabin door opened, two uniformed guards accompanied an airport worker and immigration officer as they entered the plane. The airport agent used the plane's intercom and spoke in English with a thick Spanish accent.

"¡Bienvenido! Welcome to Cuba! I am so happy you have landed safely to come to visit us." She handed the mike to the immigration officer. He instructed passengers to prepare to hand over their passports. "Señors y señoras, please hand the agent your passports. She will be collecting them for us to process. You may only take your carry-on luggage with you when you deplane. A customs officer will greet you at the bottom of the stairway and inspect your things. Also, know there will be a health inspection before you go into the airport."

Mr. Roque asked to speak to the passengers. "Hopefully this is a short stop for us and will not delay our arrival in Cayman by much. I will make arrangements for meals while we wait for the problem to be inspected by the mechanics here. If it's all good, we will be back on our way quickly. Thanks for your patience and cooperation."

Hours later, waiting in the terminal, the troupe was getting impatient. Empanadas and canned sodas, imitating Coca-Cola, were delivered to the passengers and crew. Roque and Cross were on their cell phones constantly. Finally, Mr. Roque gathered everyone around.

"It appears that the problem with our plane isn't a simple fix. We have the charter company's mechanics on their way to make repairs. Another plane is not available. So, it looks like we will be staying here for tonight. We are not permitted to offload any luggage, so you will have to stay with only what you have with you. A bus will be here to pick us up in a few minutes and take us to a hotel. Mr. Cross will go with you. I'm staying with the aircraft and pilots to deal with the repairs."

A few of the troupe were grumbling, obviously disturbed that this change of plans was upsetting their expectations of getting to the resort on Grand Cayman. Most looked to Ritiki to see her reaction. She was stoic and seemed to be handling the situation without any drama.

"We will arrange a trip to a place where you can get anything you might need for our short stay. You know, toiletries or rum." Roque smiled as he guided them to the bus.

The historic hotel was nice enough and fortunately had enough rooms to accommodate the entire group. After settling in they met in the lobby for the shopping excursion to the central square. Being close enough to walk, they formed lines like a tourist tour group and followed the hotel concierge to the square. He directed them to the stores around the plaza.

Matvey told Clara, "This feels strange. It is familiar and yet foreign to me. I used to come here from Girón when I was a child. We would walk around town and sit by the fountains just watching the people. I keep looking for faces I might know, but now I don't see anyone but the residents of a place I no longer know."

Clara said, "We have everything we need so let's just sit here and watch the world go by until we need to go back to the hotel." That was fine with Matvey. The anxiety of being in Cuba where he might be apprehended troubled him deeply. Clara knew nothing of this part of his life. He never disclosed his past as a lothario. He especially wanted to keep secret his accidental theft of the cross of Friar Bartolomé and Evelyn's bloody injury episode when she hit her head and he left her for dead. It all seemed so long ago and such a surreal nightmare.

Clara and Matvey wandered back to the hotel before the rest of the group. Along the way, they passed a group of Russians who were loading fresh provisions on a small truck, including eggs, fruits, and vegetables, and cases of Havana Club 15 rum. They were for the big yachts anchored in the harbor. A man in a chef's white coat was inspecting the produce as workers loaded crates onto the truck. A taller gentleman with graying blonde hair in a ship's steward uniform was standing aside, supervising.

Clara teased, "Matvey that man looks like you! Except he is old and fat! You better not get to look like that when you get old." As they walked past they were close enough to see his sparkling green eyes. Clara whispered, "He's even got green eyes like yours!"

Matvey frowned and looked closer at the man. Their eyes met and for a moment they stared before averting their gaze. It was unsettling for both Matvey and the ship's steward to see a reflection of themselves in each other. Matvey turned to Clara, whispering, "Let's get out of here. That guy gives me the creeps."

The next morning the group gathered for breakfast in a small meeting room. Roque and Cross made an announcement, "Ritiki and her assistant have left for Cayman on a small charter plane we arranged last night. She looks forward to you joining her there soon and appreciates your flexibility and patience with this unforeseen situation."

Cross continued, "We will be here another night. We need to stick close together and not get in any trouble here in Cuba that might cause further complications. So please stay in the hotel or go no farther than the plaza. The mechanics have returned to Miami to get parts for the repairs, but they must return through Nassau due to the U.S. embargo on Cuba. That delays things a bit, but they assured us the fix was simple if they have the correct parts. We are sorry for the delay."

Roque was back to business, "You know this puts us a little behind in our dress rehearsals for our demonstration. I'm sure you are all very well prepared for this and we should be able to get back on schedule a day ahead of the show. Does anybody have any questions?"

Hector raised his hand, "Mr. Roque, why can't we get our luggage? It would be better than having to wear the same clothes for three days!"

"Well, there are two problems. One is that the Cuban authorities have requested us not to disembark our luggage without unloading the entire cargo. Secondly, since our gear is packed with our luggage, it presents a chance for damage or, more concerning, inspectors might pilfer essential items. I also trust that there isn't anything packed in your suitcases that would be prohibited in Cuba and perhaps confiscated."

His answer seemed to calm the concern over the luggage. The troupe members could suffer through the inconvenience of not having their personal belongings for another day. Soon enough they would be in the high-end resort in George Town and able to begin work on their reason for being in the Caymans, to make Ritiki a star as big as the sun, and, along the way, make themselves celebrities too.

TWENTY-SIX

The Cuban immigration officer, Miguel, had all of the passports and was processing the group's entry. Everything was in order until he checked the computer notes where he found Matvey's Cuban passport had been flagged. The note on the file indicated he was wanted for an unspecified "crime against the Revolution," and advised that he should be detained. Any immigration or customs officer should contact Agent Oscar Fernández of the G2 Unit in the General Directorate of Intelligence or Detective Inspector Carlos Costa of the Cienfuegos Police Department.

This surprised Miguel and he conferred with his supervisor. "Marielisa, look what I found! What should we do?"

Marielisa Gutiérrez replied sharply. "Miguel, what does it say to do?! We must call the contacts and refer this to them. First, call the G2. They are the most powerful authority and we need to keep them from getting upset with us."

Miguel said, "I mean about detaining this person. He is no longer here in the airport."

"Oh." She thought for a moment. "I think we know where he is, so let's just let the authorities make the decision. I don't think we need to apprehend their suspect and cause a problem that is over our head."

Miguel called the number for Fernández and got a recording that the phone was no longer in service. Then he tried the number for Costa in Cienfuegos.

Inspector Costa was back to his usual routine of investigating thefts, drug trafficking, and assaults, usually the result of domestic disputes. Serious crimes were unusual but not unknown in Cuba. The harsh intolerance for criminal activity kept a lid on most serious, anti-social behavior.

Costa answered the phone, "Detective Inspector Carlos Costa. What can I do to assist?"

"My name is Miguel with the Immigration Department. I am at the Cienfuegos airport. Yesterday a charter flight from Nassau to Cayman diverted here to make an emergency landing due to mechanical problems. The plane is still here awaiting repair."

Costa interrupted, "I think you have the wrong number. This is the Cienfuegos Police Department. You should call the Aviation Ministry about this."

"No sir, it is not about the plane, but one of the passengers. He is with a group of musical performers. I am processing their passports."

Before Miguel even finished his sentence, a thought shot through Costa's sharp mind, "This is about Matvey Descon! How could it be? I am so lucky if fate brought him to me instead of chasing him in the U.S. or Bahamas!"

Miguel continued, "The name is Matvey Descon. The note on the passport file said to contact G2 agent Oscar Fernández or you if he was encountered. The note also said to apprehend him for crimes. Because we only collected passports in this emergency, he left the airport with the group to stay here in Cienfuegos until the plane is repaired. We do not have him in custody."

Costa was quick to answer, "Agent Fernández is no longer in the country or with G2. I can handle this. Where do you think he is staying?"

"I'm not sure, but I think I heard one of the men say 'La Union' but I really don't know."

Costa was pleased at this lead. He thanked Miguel effusively for his assistance. "You did a good service for Cuba. You may keep his passport," adding, with smug sarcasm, "You may give it back to him if he ever returns to board the plane."

TWENTY-SEVEN

General Rodolfo Diego arrived at the Girón Beach Club Resort with his entourage. He planned to stay at the resort until his meeting with the Russians and other top officials of the Republic. Maria, the general manager since the Soviets departed, greeted him warmly as a familiar guest. His usual suite was available. For a long time, he had been meeting his girlfriend at the resort, well away from his wife at home in Havana.

The general invited Maria to have a rum in his suite. The soldier guards were stationed outside. His trusted aide joined them.

"Maria, I have some big news for you! I am here for a meeting with a bunch of rich Russians who travel around the world on their big ships. They are here to look at a place they can develop into a safe port. One of the places they are considering is right here on the Bay of Pigs."

Maria was astounded at this news. General Diego was bursting with the need to tell someone and get accolades for his prominent role in the negotiations. She was a safe pair of ears and he trusted her discretion. He was busting to boast about his involvement. She said, "Oh my God, that is really big news. What does it mean for Girón Beach Club Resort?"

The General continued, "If they choose this site, they will build a new private resort just for them. The townspeople would have jobs in the new compound, but there would be no tourists. It would be different." As an afterthought, he added, "I'm sure you would be an, or *the*, important manager, just like you became the manager after the Soviet 'El Jefe' ran away back to Russia."

Maria recoiled at the general's tone when he mentioned Ivan Volkov. She had been infatuated with Volkov and would have done anything for him. But he seemed to prefer Juanita, the dancer instead of her. To General Diego she said, "Ivan Volkov did not want to leave. He had to go."

Diego replied, "Yes, of course. All of the Russians had to leave when the Soviet Union dissolved and abandoned Cuba." He added, "You should look to the future and what this new investment might mean for you."

Maria was relieved to know that she would have a future if this plan moved forward.

General Diego continued, "One of the problems is that there is no protected place for their large yachts to anchor at Girón. They might develop a harbor at Playa Larga, but it's a little far away. These people have so much money, they can do anything, anywhere. They seem focused on an island spot near the Ensenada de Guabina on Cienfuegos Bay. No matter. Our military conglomerate owns both places, so whatever they do will be good for us and Cuba. Of course, please keep this to yourself. I will let you know what happens at our meeting."

Maria assured him that her lips were sealed as she made a gesture of locking her lips. She smiled, "I am so honored you shared this with me."

"Well, it is time for me to relax and prepare for bed. Thank you for coming. As always you are welcoming and take good care of me. I have a big day tomorrow. I will be meeting with one of the Castro family and the ambassador to The Bahamas, Dr. António Montañez, who has been working to secure the investment of the Russians."

TWENTY-EIGHT

Because Ritiki's troupe would be staying in Cuba another day Matvey had an opportunity he never imagined he would ever have. He could visit his mother's grave. It was not far from Cienfuegos, less than an hour's trip by car. He wondered, "Can I risk this? I'll never have another chance."

Talking with Clara, she reluctantly agreed he could go. It was against the rules set by Cross and Roque. He explained to Clara, "It should only take a couple hours at most. But, in Cuba, one never knows what delays could happen. So, it might be late, even overnight, but I should be back no later than first thing in the morning." Having enough U.S. dollars in his pocket, Matvey took a taxi to the nearby resort town of Playa Girón.

The cab driver was more than happy to take this strange looking Cuban, with American dollars, to his destination. He would even wait for this man if it meant he'd get more U.S. currency.

Standing at her graveside, Matvey bawled. He fell to his knees at her grave. He loved his mother and missed her terribly. "Why did she have to die so young? She was so beautiful and kind," he said through his tears.

After a few minutes, Matvey regained his composure and began remembering his childhood at the Girón Beach Club Resort. He had so many questions that would never be answered. He spoke from his heart to the simple marker in the town cemetery.

Addressing the simple headstone, Matvey said, "My beloved Mother, I love you and I miss you so much. I wish we were together. I have so many questions. Why did you never tell me about my father? I saw the photos of you when you were young and at the dance academy in Havana. But why did he leave you? I know nothing of him or his family or even his family name. Should I hate him for leaving us in Girón?

"It was such a happy time for me at the resort. Everyone was so nice, except Maria. Why did you hate her so much? She was good to me after you were gone, like she was my mother, from a distance. But you hated her. I don't understand."

Matvey was sniffling with tear-filled eyes.

"I want to tell you about my life and my new love, Clara. I had to leave Cuba and almost died in a hurricane trying to reach the U.S. But, it has all worked out OK for me. People helped me survive and now I am here with you again, even if only for a moment.

"And, then there's Clara. She is from Puerto Rico. She is beautiful and smart. I love her and will ask her to marry me. We work at a resort in The Bahamas. It is something like our beach club was but much more exclusive.

"I am also a professional dancer. You taught me well. I remember all the lessons and performing with you at the poolside. A big star in the Caribbean asked me to dance with her at a party where I was a waiter. Then, she asked me to join her troupe because I am such a good dancer. I danced with her at big concerts all over – in Columbia, Venezuela, Mexico, and even in Miami!"

Matvey sat on the grass, just staring at the headstone. Startled from his trance, he heard footsteps. Two uniformed police and a man in street clothes were walking toward him. The taxi waiting for him was driving away.

He blinked in disbelief. Matvey recognized the man. It was Inspector Costa! Matvey leaped to his feet, kicking over the bundle of wildflowers he had collected for his mother. The officers grabbed him and forcefully held him immobile while Costa spoke.

"Matvey Valdez Descon, you are under arrest for your crimes. I have you this time and you shall not get away!" The officers cuffed him and manhandled him into the back of the police car. Costa followed closely behind, so gratified and proud that this fugitive would finally be facing justice for assault at Girón and the theft of the Cross of the Friar Bartolomé religious artifact from the archives in Havana.

Matvey offered no resistance. He said nothing on the ride back to Cienfuegos. He knew he was captured and it was hopeless.

Arriving at the jail, Costa escorted him to a private cell. He would be detained apart for the riffraff in the main holding cell. Costa did not want anything to happen to Matvey, at least not until he could be presented as a trophy to General Diego.

Matvey surveyed his new accommodations. Austere and depressing, the cell was dark, with only a little light streaming in from small windows high over the floor. The dank odor of human bodies, mixed with the musty odor of the enclosed space, permeated the hot humid atmosphere. A wooden bench was bolted to the wall. A bucket for use as a toilet was hanging on a hook along with a small rag. Light streamed through a barred window high overhead. The rusted bars were worn smooth where countless detainees had grabbed the strong steel grate.

Matvey thought, "What a dilemma I am in now. Nobody knows where I am and I can't call Clara. She must be worried. Roque and Cross will be very angry when I don't show up." He closed his eyes and leaned his head back against the wall, despondent over his situation. "Nobody can get me out of this predicament. There is no escape."

The cell across the hall from him was crowded with men being held for processing. Some were pacing back and forth. A few leaned on the bars searching the hallway for someone to come. It had only been an hour since Costa deposited him in this cell and yet it felt like forever.

TWENTY-NINE

With several cruise ship-sized yachts in Cienfuegos Bay, tenders were zipping back and forth to the dock. Located on the south side of the island, the bay is perhaps Cuba's best natural port. It is a large inlet connected to the Caribbean Sea through a narrow canal. The water is deep enough for cargo ships and, over the years, industrial development grew along with the city, now with a population of 180,000 or more.

The historic city square is both the town center geographically and culturally. The open plaza and park is a public space where residents can gather and relax. The city boasts several museums, including the Casa-Taller Santiago Hermes Art Gallery with a wonderful, if somewhat stale, collection.

Captive on her husband's giant yacht, Evelyn didn't want for anything except a little freedom and a chance to walk in the Cuba she loved. Her former role as an art professor, tour leader, and, sometimes, art trafficker was indeed in her past. She still appreciated the visual arts and visited galleries and museums at every chance. In her position as a wealthy patron versus an academic art historian, her visits to galleries were now from a different perspective. And, as an oligarch's wife, she always had a security detail.

Since it had been several years since she visited the Hermes museum, she decided to go ashore. She informed her husband, "I would like to go to the Hermes Museum in the city."

Klotchkof told her, "That's nice dear. But, I can't go with you. I am busy. I have planned a dinner aboard tonight. The chef has to arrange for some local supplies so we can have a Cuban-themed menu. Take your security with you and keep in touch. The steward, Ivan Volkov, can make the arrangements. Just don't dally. Tonight is too important and I want you by my side!"

Evelyn leaned over her husband and kissed his forehead in a touching gesture of affection.

Klotchkof repeated, "Evelyn, my sweetheart, consult with Volkov before you go to the town. He worked here in Cuba at a resort. Maybe, he can give you some advice on where to go. And, take security!"

Evelyn really didn't need any information on where to go in Cienfuegos. Her husband was aware that she had been to Havana for research and leading art tours for her students from Britain. But, he did not know how extensively she had traveled throughout the country.

In addition to the historic town of Trinidad, this community was one of her favorite places. The town was not so focused on the tourist trade and did not seem as deteriorated as many other cities in Cuba, especially the non-tourist areas of Havana.

She boarded a tender for the trip to the Cienfuegos Yacht Club dock. From there it was a short walk to the museum. To the locals, she and her security detail were obvious visitors, even with her guards wearing tropical-colored traditional guayabera shirts to better assimilate into the local traffic. Evelyn stood out anywhere, being tall, blonde, and beautiful, dressed in a designer outfit.

Strolling the streets, she breathed in deeply, savoring the fragrances of the city, both the foul air and the pleasant smells of bakeries, restaurants, and the flowering landscape. Occasionally, the aroma of cigars wafted from the men playing dominoes or chess at small tables in the plaza. Evelyn enjoyed her brief visit to the city. The gallery was as she remembered. A couple of temporary exhibits refreshed the permanent collection.

She was almost at the Yacht Club on her way back to the tender when a car abruptly made a U-turn in the wide street and came to a panicked stop in front of her. Her security team was immediately piqued and moved quickly to protect their charge.

The driver opened his door and called out to her, "Dr. Evelyn Kaye Griffin! I thought I recognized you! What a surprise! You are here in Cienfuegos! Do you remember me? I'm your old friend Carlos Costa! Do you have a minute?"

Costa could not believe his good fortune to find both Matvey and Evelyn in his city. Evelyn stopped to face the person calling out to her. It took a few seconds for her to displace her anxiety about Costa and remember she was now at a level beyond the reach of Cuban law enforcement.

Responding to the hail, Evelyn said, "Oh yes! How could I forget your kindness when I was last in Cuba?"

A policeman got out of the passenger side of the car and moved with Costa to approach Evelyn. As they moved closer one of her guards overreacted and grabbed the officer, throwing him to the ground. Costa tried to pull the strong guard off his uniformed officer and was stopped by Evelyn's other two bodyguards. When the police officer rose to his feet, pulling his nightstick from his belt, the guard resumed slamming him to the concrete street curb. It was horrifying to hear his arm bone snap and the officer howl in pain. Once the officer was injured and presumed to no longer be a threat, the aggressive protection by her guard detail eased.

During the entire violent episode, Evelyn screamed in English and Russian, "Stop! Stop! Do not hurt them. Dimitri! Stop!" The entire incident happened quickly and was over in a matter of seconds. Evelyn reasoned that Dimitri thought there was a threat even though the officer was in uniform. It was lucky that the Russian guards were not armed, having been instructed to sequester their firearms while in Cuba, or the situation might have been even worse. She retreated to a nearby bench, surrounded by her guards, and waited.

Costa rushed to his injured officer and radioed for an emergency responder. When an ambulance arrived, the injured officer was quickly transported to the emergency hospital. More police cars arrived, with a dozen cops, responding to the assault on their brother. Costa asked them to keep an eye on the guards but to stand down and not engage.

Costa asked Evelyn if they could have a brief private conversation, away from the gathering crowd of spectators. She agreed, not wanting any further escalation or any more violent confrontation on what was supposed to be a pleasant shoreside excursion.

Evelyn directed her guards, saying in Russian, "It will be OK." She signaled a hand gesture indicating they should wait for her where they were. The other two bodyguards restrained their coworker while the Cienfuegos police surrounded the area.

Costa and Evelyn walked to a landscaped garden alcove with a bench overlooking the bay. She could see her husband's yacht out in the harbor. "Inspector Costa, it's nice to see you. I deeply apologize for the altercation between your officer and my security guard. He was only trying to protect me. I truly hope your man is not badly injured."

Costa responded, "I think his arm is broken and he hit his head. Your man is obviously a professional and strong. We can discuss the attack later. First, I have a few questions."

Evelyn stated, "I am in a new position. That is my husband's yacht out there," as she pointed it out. "He's a very wealthy Russian businessman here to make a high-level deal with your government." Now that she had stated that Costa could not legally detain her, she offered, "What can I help you with?"

Realizing Evelyn was now politically connected, all Costa could do was satisfy his curiosity about events that happened in the past. He said, "When you escaped...err...left Cuba we issued an international arrest warrant for you, which I assume you somehow evaded back in England. Now you are back in Cuba. We should take you into custody on charges of art trafficking, but I think with your new status and obvious government connections it would be a waste of our time."

"Yes, it likely would be. You see," as she opened her purse and retrieved her passport, "I am now a dual citizen of the United Kingdom and Russia and this addendum to my passport shows my status as having diplomatic immunity. Besides, I think the people my husband is negotiating with would not be pleased if his wife were incarcerated." Her wry smile harkened back to Costa's manipulation and gamesmanship with her when she was under suspicion of art trafficking years ago.

"Oh, I see. Exactly. At least we have your accomplice Professor Yolanda Lopez-Ballar in prison. It looks like we have one of your co-conspirators paying for your crime."

"Oh no! Please! Inspector Costa, I can tell you now because you can't do anything to me. Yolanda was nothing but a kind and generous friend. She had nothing to do with my activities in the art world. She was assigned to accompany me while I was at the archives. She was merely caught up in trying to help me when I was injured and in the hospital. Please tell me what I can do to exonerate her. She does not deserve to be in jail. She was, no, she *is* a saint and a total professional."

Costa said, "Really?" He paused. "If that is true, I will do my best to get Professor Lopez-Ballar released and cleared, but you must tell me the complete story." Smugly sniping at her, he continued, "Now that you are beyond the reach of the law!"

Evelyn took a breath, "I had been coming to Cuba to research art for many years, since my days in graduate school. I found I could pay for my studies if I found valuable art to sell. I got involved in acquiring vintage paintings and taking them out of Cuba to sell in American and European galleries. The theft of the Crucifix de Friar Bartolomé was an accident."

Costa was surprised. "It was *you* who stole the cross?"

He was perplexed, wondering how Matvey ended up with the artifact. "So it was not Matvey who stole the gold cross?"

Evelyn shook her head, "No, originally it was me, but I never intended to. It was a mistake."

Costa raised his eyebrows as he exclaimed, "What?! How could it be a mistake?"

"Let me explain. I was at the archives going through the files of artwork from before and after the Revolution, doing legitimate research. When I was left alone, I started looking around. I opened a drawer of artifacts and pulled out the Crucifix de Friar Bartolomé. I knew the history of the hallowed 16th-century friar called the "Protector of the Indians." The cross was so beautiful and such a tangible connection to the priest who devoted his life to fighting for the humane treatment of the indigenous natives. I only wanted to look at it more closely. Then I heard footsteps in the hall.

"Before I could put it back, the drawer shut and was locked. When I was discovered in the room, I hid it in my blouse and smuggled it out of the building. I had no intention of stealing the cross but I couldn't put it back. I panicked and took the it. I didn't know what else to do.

"Then I traveled to Girón to hide until I could leave the island. I met a young man, a great dancer I might add, at the resort. He and I had a … ah … an intimate evening, late into the night. I discovered him holding the cross from where I had it hidden. We struggled. When I got tangled up in my bathrobe I tripped and must have hit my head and been knocked out." She raised the bangs on her forehead to reveal the faint scar from the laceration. "I have no idea what happened to the crucifix. I do know the guy who took it from me is in The Bahamas now."

Costa was happy to have the details filled in even though he couldn't do anything about it. "Well, you will be happy to know that Matvey Valdez Descon, the thief and your assailant is not in The Bahamas. He is in custody right here in Cienfuegos. I've got him in a private cell awaiting prosecution."

Evelyn was surprised. "What? That's incredible."

"Yes, Descon arrived here on an airplane that landed due to an emergency mechanical problem. When it's repaired, I guess they will be leaving without him. Also, you should know the cross was recovered and is back in the national archives again." Costa was proud of his persistence in following this case.

"I am happy that the cross has been repatriated. It is an important piece of your country's history. It shouldn't be lost or even hidden in an archive drawer. Like I said, it was not my intention to steal it."

Costa was unimpressed, as Evelyn continued to excuse her thievery. "Really, I just didn't know what else to do." Changing the subject, she asked, "What will happen to Matvey?"

"Perhaps he will face severe punishment. He has angered some very powerful people in the military and intelligence agency. They may lock him up and throw away the key. I don't care. My job was to apprehend him for stealing a national treasure and assaulting you, even though it turns out you had stolen the cross from the archives. Stealing, even from a thief, is a crime."

Evelyn was a little saddened to learn this, even though she still resented Matvey for stealing the cross from her. The night they spent together was very sensual until things went wrong. Now she was in a better circumstance and it appeared Matvey had been too. Although their crimes were now catching up with them, they seemed distantly in the past.

She said to Costa, "This man, Matvey, might have stolen the crucifix from me, but he did not assault me. His only crime was 'seduction' of a vulnerable woman."

Costa said, "Thank you for helping me understand. Now, unfortunately, I need to address what your guard did to the officer. I can't let that go. Assaulting the police is something I cannot overlook. I'm afraid he will have to be arrested until we can figure out what to do."

"I understand. I don't speak much Russian, but I will tell him he must go with you and cooperate until we can get him out of jail."

The two returned to where the guards and contingent of police were waiting. The crowds had dissipated somewhat since there was not much to see except police standing around three casually-dressed Russian men.

Evelyn explained to Dimitri that he needed to comply and wait patiently until she could arrange for his return to the boat. He submitted to the police and was handcuffed to be transported to the jail. Once there, the fellow police officers treated him very roughly and pushed him into the holding cell which was crowded with unsavory crime suspects. His hand-to-hand defense skills kept him safe from being attacked by the other detainees. Not speaking Spanish, he was alone, accepting that he would have to wait for someone from the ship to come for him.

Evelyn shook hands with Costa. "You are a good man, Inspector. And, I respect your efforts to investigate my crime. But for now, let's part with mutual respect as worthy adversaries and call it a truce, OK?"

Costa agreed, "Yes, a truce. You are a crafty, resourceful woman … and so beautiful. Good luck in your new reformed life."

As she walked away, Carlos shouted, "Oh, I almost forgot, I still have your crate of artwork in our evidence room. Do you want it?"

Evelyn turned and walked a few steps back toward him, "Oh! No. Thank you. My walls are full. I have no more space for art. Please send it to the Hermes Museum. There might be some works of interest for their collection," she smiled. "The art pieces belong in a Cuban gallery." She turned away and did not look back.

Inspector Costa watched Evelyn and two of her bodyguards return to the launch at the Yacht Club and motor out to her ship. He was gratified to have her confession, albeit without being able to act on it. He considered how he could get Yolanda cleared. He scribbled a note on the pad he kept in his pocket. Costa's concern then shifted to his deputy and getting to the hospital to check on his condition.

Evelyn returned to the boat and explained to her husband what had happened. She didn't disclose the past events with Matvey at Girón. She had met her husband in her role as an art trafficker so her interaction with Costa about a crime wasn't a problem for her to explain. He could look past the reason Costa had stopped her on the street. On the other hand, her husband was very angry with her guard.

"That man can rot in a Cuban jail for all I care! It was completely undisciplined for him to attack a policeman without better justification than that he might be a threat to you. I do not want this incident to spoil our congenial relationship with the Cubans. They probably don't care about it, and it won't derail this negotiation, but …. goddamn, I have higher expectations."

"My darling Nikolai, he was only trying to protect me!"

"Yes, I suppose. I'm glad you are safe and it is better that he acted than you were hurt. In reality, I suppose it could have been an assassin disguised as a Cuban cop." He laughed at the implausibility.

THIRTY

The hospital was crowded with patients and their friends and family in the waiting area. Costa registered with the desk and asked to speak with the doctors treating his officer. A nurse told him, "You will have to wait."

He went outside to wait, using the time to call Fernández to tell him the good news that Matvey was in custody. Fernández was astounded by the good fortune of capturing Matvey in Girón and learning that it was Evelyn, not Matvey, who stole the cross from the National Archives. But it did not change the fact that Matvey had the religious relic in his possession on the beach in the Dry Tortugas. He was still a thief.

"Congratulations my friend. You have accomplished in just a few hours what we have been chasing for a long time. And, he's now right there in Cienfuegos! What good luck it was that the plane he was on had mechanical problems. But Girón is not Cienfuegos where he was supposed to be at a hotel. How did you find him in Girón?"

Costa explained, "I found the hotel where the group was staying. I planned to arrest him there but as I drove up, I saw a tall blond guy get in a cab. It could only have been the criminal we have been looking for for so long. I decided to follow him. If I made a mistake in identity I would find out when the guy reached his destination. But when the cab turned to head to Girón I knew I had the right man. When the cab reached the cemetery I waited to see what he was up to and called for a couple more of my officers to join me. I guess he needed to see someone there. When he got up to leave I arrested him! Imagine his surprise to see me!"

Fernández replied "What is it they say, 'The criminal always returns to the site of the crime.'"

Costa laughed. "Dónde estás? Where are you now?"

"I am in Havana. As it happens I am on my way to Cienfuegos. There is a secret meeting there with Russians to develop a port for their big boats. I don't know the details. My boss, the ambassador, is very involved in the negotiations. And The General will be there with other officials of the government."

Costa said, "I'm aware of this. Our harbor is full of big luxury yachts. There's a lot of security people here. Theirs and ours. I think the meeting is tomorrow. I'm at the hospital now. One of their big goons attacked the officer who was with me when I interviewed Evelyn. Evelyn was the woman Matvey assaulted in Girón. It's a long story. It's complicated."

"When I get there we can celebrate and you can give me the whole story. I've got to go now. The ambassador is ready to leave."

"OK, my friend. But I have an idea I want to talk to you about. Adiós."

Costa then went back to the front doors of the hospital and using his badge, he pushed his way through the crowded lobby to the nurse's station. He flashed his badge at the receptionist at the desk and demanded to know the status of his comrade. "I am Inspector Costa of the Cienfuegos police. I must speak with the doctor treating my officer."

The receptionist called someone. "A nurse will come and take you to the ward."

Costa learned that his deputy had a severe fracture that would require surgery. Both bones in his arm had snapped when he landed on the street curb. Stone is stronger than bone. The busy physician briskly told Costa, "He has a bad break. We will operate as soon as the orthopedist gets here. Please be patient, as we are very busy. Wait."

Costa was concerned and phoned the station to tell them he would be at the hospital indefinitely.

THIRTY-ONE

Evelyn gave her husband a few minutes to simmer down about Dimitri's mistake. She asked. "I know my bodyguard made a big mistake to attack the policeman, but can't we do something to help him out of this?'

He snapped, "No, I'm not even inclined to get him a return flight to Russia. His actions threaten my agenda."

"I was thinking that maybe we could at least get him out of jail. May I call to see if I can help?"

"Fine, just don't make a bigger mess, and definitely do not go to the shore to do anything. Stay on the boat!"

Evelyn retreated to her study. She found General Diego's contact information, and called him, catching him on his way from Girón to Cienfuegos to attend the meeting with her husband and his colleagues.

"General, I am Evelyn Klotchkof. We met in The Bahamas and you are meeting with my husband tomorrow. I need your help with a problem."

Like all men, he wanted to solve a lady's problems. He also thought doing a favor for the wife of the oligarch would ingratiate him and leverage some goodwill for the negotiations.

"Yes, of course. What can I do for you?"

Evelyn explained the unfortunate incident when she was detained by the local police, not revealing it was about her past involvement in criminal activities. "It was all a mistake, by the police and my security guard. Now my guard has been arrested and I think he is in the local jail, or police station. I really don't know where."

General Diego replied. "Do not worry about this anymore. I will get him for you. Where can I return him to you?"

"Maybe at the Yacht Club dock. I can send a launch to pick him up there. If you can do this for me, I will be very appreciative, and I assure you that there will be no more trouble from him or anyone else on our boat."

THIRTY-TWO

General Diego directed his motorcade to go to the central station of the Cienfuegos police. His parade of vehicles parked at the entrance. Along with a half dozen armed commandos, his assistant approached the duty officer. "The general needs to see the commander of this station! Now!"

The duty officer was overwhelmed by the unusual circumstance of a general and entourage standing there making demands. He managed to get his thoughts together and say, "Most of our force is out patrolling and securing locations for a big event that is happening tomorrow. The chief is directing them and unavailable."

General Diego interrupted, "I want to see whoever is in charge here. I have a prisoner I need to retrieve. You are holding a Russian from one of the boats in the harbor. Is he here?"

The duty officer flipped through some papers and asked a nearby officer to take General Diego to the holding cells. "Officer Reyes will guide you. Please follow him."

The procession snaked through the old building, down flights of stairs, and through dark hallways. They came upon a locked steel door. The guard seated by the side of the door was startled by the approach of armed men and an army general.

General Diego snapped at the guard, "I am here to take custody of a prisoner. He is a Russian named Dimitri something. Get him now!"

Timidly, the guard asked, "Sir, do you have transfer papers? I can't …"

The general barked, "¡Mierda! I do not need transfer papers! Do you know who I am? I am General Rodolfo Diego, the senior general of the Revolutionary Army. Take me to him now!"

The guard trembled as he unlocked the door and took the general to the dimly lit hall lined with cells. General Diego demanded, "Which one is the Russian?" as he looked at the crowded cells filled with perpetrators waiting for processing.

The guard did not know. Diego turned around and looked at a cell opposite the ones with many men within. This cell had a single occupant who was seated on a bench in the corner. The man was larger than the average Cuban, blonde, and dressed in nice clothes.

"I am General Diego. I am here to get you and return you to your boat!" The man said nothing, only looking up with astonishment in his green eyes.

Matvey didn't know who this army general was or why he was in the jail making demands. But, whatever was going on, he could see that this was an opportunity to get out of jail, if he played the part. He would figure out how to get back to Clara and the others if only he could get out of the cell. He didn't move until the general's assistant asked, "¿Hablas español?"

Matvey answered a quiet "Nyet." It was one of the few Russian words he had learned long ago at the Girón Beach Club Resort. He would say nothing more because the only other phrase he knew was "Dasvidaniya."

The general was satisfied he had located the lady's bodyguard. At General Diego's command, "This man!", the guard unlocked the metal grate and two of the general's soldiers took him by the arms to lead him away, out of the cell block. The general's final orders to the guard were, "Say nothing about this until after tomorrow. Do you understand?"

The police officer and the cell guard nodded in agreement. It would be hard to explain this to their superiors. They were happy to delay informing them until later.

The general directed his men to place their prisoner in the supply truck that was following the motorcade. "Keep him under guard until we drop him off at the Yacht Club. I will call to let someone know they may pick him up." He then left a voicemail message for Evelyn.

They deposited their prisoner at the Yacht Club and told him to wait for the boat. Matvey understood what they were saying, but feigned to not speak Spanish. The general was late for his scheduled appointment with other government officials who would be participating in the negotiations tomorrow. He left quickly, not waiting to be sure Matvey was on the launch.

Matvey smiled and waved as the entourage left, shouting his thank you. "Dasvidaniya!" and, under his breath, "Muchas gracias!"

As soon as they were gone, Matvey rushed back to the hotel. A bus was waiting on the street at the front of the hotel.

As Matvey approached, Cross yelled, "Where the hell have you been? What is it with you? Always a problem!"

Matvey ducked his head in deference to Cross' admonishment and boarded the bus.

Clara said, "I was worried when you didn't come back quickly. It took a long time for you to go to your mother's grave. I thought we might leave without you. But, you are here now and that's all that matters. Mr. Cross is still looking for Hector and Nigel. I have your things so you don't need to go back to our room."

Matvey was happy that Mr. Cross was distracted with concern for the whereabouts of Nigel and Hector. It took the pressure off of explaining where he had been.

In a few minutes, Nigel and Hector sauntered up to the hotel. Cross berated them for being out. "Our mechanic has the plane ready to go, ahead of schedule. So get on the bus!"

Nigel offered an excuse. "We were detained by a Cuban policeman for a little while. He saw us holding hands and wanted to hassle us. He did not like any public display of affection. I guess he must not have heard about the Castro family deciding to tolerate homosexuality since one of their own is queer. Now in Cuba, gay is OK."

Hector asked, "Can I go to my room and get my backpack?"

Cross shouted, "Hurry!" He was clearly anxious to get on the way to the airport and the waiting plane.

Finally, with all of the cast and crew on board the bus, they departed for the airport. The same immigration officer that had welcomed them was there to process their exit, handing each passenger their passports. All was going smoothly until it was Matvey's turn.

Miguel stated, as he looked at the passport photo and then at Matvey to compare the picture, "Sir, there was a note about you being detained."

Matvey presented an inquisitive innocent face. "Really?"

"The police officer I spoke with said not to return your passport unless you came back. You are here, so I guess I can give it back to you." Miguel smiled as he handed the booklet back to Matvey.

Matvey climbed the stairs and took his seat next to Clara. He was eager to go and get in the air, out of reach of the Cuban authorities. The cabin door closed and the captain announced they would be taking off soon and on the ground on Grand Cayman in about an hour. "I apologize again for our delay here in Cuba. I hope you had some time to enjoy the hospitality and culture of Cienfuegos."

The plane taxied down the runway and paused waiting for the air traffic controllers to authorize their departure. Only a few minutes passed but Matvey felt it was hours. At any time, his escape could be discovered. Clara held his arm and asked, "Why are you so nervous? Is flying a problem? I'm sure they fixed the airplane."

Matvey sighed, "No, I am just wanting to leave Cuba. It's no longer my home!"

Clara patted his arm reassuringly, "We will go soon."

Feeling the plane rise into the sky and hearing the wheels retract, Matvey exhaled with relief. He had had enough of the hospitality and the culture of his home country. Soon he would be in the Cayman Islands and, in a few more days, back at Callaloo.

He looked out the window to see Cienfuegos below and Girón in the distance. He whispered to himself. "Fairwell my beloved country. I hope to never see you again . . . if I am lucky. And, today, I am feeling very lucky!

THIRTY-THREE

Carlos Costa's cell phone announced the call from Fernández. "Hola, where are you? I am still at the hospital. My officer has just had surgery. The surgeon says his repair was successful and he should recover."

"I'm with the ambassador. We just arrived in Cienfuegos. I'm sorry, but I let it slip that you had captured Matvey. The ambassador phoned General Diego immediately. They made plans to go to the police station to meet this infamous criminal. As you know, the ambassador did not want him to be an embarrassment in The Bahamas. But being arrested here in Cuba eliminates any problems in Nassau."

Costa asked his friend, "Do you know The General's reaction?"

"The ambassador told me he could not tell if Diego was peeved or pleased. He was gruff and rude, as usual," replied Fernández.

Costa responded, "Oh. When are they going to the prison? I want to meet them there. Maybe we can convince the general to get you reinstated with G2 and you can come back to Cuba. That is what I wanted to discuss with you, the reason I called you. I was going to call Diego after we talked, but I guess that has already been taken care of by Ambassador Montañez."

"No, I don't think I'd like to be back in Cuba and with G2 again. There is a slogan the tourism ministry uses in Nassau… 'It's better in The Bahamas!' I think it's true. It is for me. I like my job with the ambassador. You asked when the general and the ambassador would meet. 30 minutes from now. Can you make it?"

"Yes, of course. I'm not far. I will be there! See you soon my friend! I can't wait for Matvey to see you again!" Costa did not know that Fernández's and Matvey's paths had already crossed at Callaloo. Fernández replied, smugly, "He will be very surprised to see me again!"

Costa pulled up just as General Diego's motorcade arrived. The ambassador and Fernández were waiting on the steps at the door to the police station. Costa raced up the stairs to meet the general. The station chief opened the door to welcome them to the Cienfuegos Police Headquarters. Although he did not like the general, he recognized the prominence of his visitors.

The chief said, "Let me introduce Detective Inspector Carlos Costa. It is through his excellent police work that he captured the thief of antiquities and a dangerous criminal. Let him guide you down to our cell block where the thief is being held."

Costa said, "Earlier today I found Matvey in a cemetery in Girón. It is through the diligence of former G2 agent Fernández flagging his passport for detention if he ever set foot on Cuban soil that led to his arrest. We are holding him here awaiting transfer to Havana for the Interior Ministry to prosecute." Extending his hand to indicate the direction they should go, he added, "Please follow me to the cell where we are holding him."

They all walked down the stairs and through the hallways. The general did not disclose that he had been there earlier to release the Russian bodyguard.

The guard at the metal door jumped up from his seat and saluted the distinguished guests. Quickly unlocking the door, it creaked open and banged the wall. The sound echoed through the cell block. The noise from the prisoners quieted as the visitors entered the dank corridor between the cells.

Costa stopped just short of the cell where he had placed Matvey to let General Diego and Ambassador Montañez stand at the front of the barred door. They were both looking in the opposite direction at the men crowded into the opposite cell. They did not know which of the prisoners was Matvey Valdez Descon.

The General asked, "Which one is the infamous criminal you have been chasing for so long?"

Costa, still not seeing that the cell he had placed Matvey in was empty, announced, "He is not with those men, he is behind you in this cell." At that moment he gestured to the empty cell and immediately recognized it was vacant.

His heart sank. He searched the adjacent cell in a panic. "I do not understand. How could this happen? He was here in this cell! Guard! GUARD come here!"

The guard at the door scurried to Costa. "Where is the occupant of this cell?" Costa demanded. "Did you move him?"

"I am so sorry sir, but I released him to the custody of General Diego earlier today - maybe a few hours ago?"

The general argued, "That was the Russian bodyguard, not a Cuban! He was tall with green eyes and blonde hair. He is on the Russian oligarch's ship by now."

Costa placed both hands over his face and rubbed his eyes. "Sir, that was Matvey Valdez Descon, who has evaded capture in Florida, Nassau, and now Cienfuegos! The Russian bodyguard is that man, over there. He is on the bench in the pink guayabera shirt." He pointed to a short muscular man with a shaved head in the crowded cell. "HE is the Russian!"

Fernández saw the humor in this situation. After he and Costa had been so demeaned by the general for their failure in capturing Matvey, the general himself had set Matvey free. He could barely avoid laughing out loud.

The station chief apologized for the failure to keep Matvey incarcerated. The general knew it was his mistake but he sharply rebuked the chief and the guard for letting the prisoner go. The ambassador intervened and politely reminded the general that the Cienfuegos police had had the prisoner secured and it was on his authority that he was released.

"General Diego, please know this was a mistake anyone could make. We all make mistakes." It was a dig at the general's complaints about the ambassador arranging for Matvey's passport. The ambassador continued, "Don't blame yourself."

General Diego buried his internal rage within his gut, knowing there was little he could do to find someone else to blame for assuming that he had the right man, who looked like a Russian, and setting him free. They all returned up the stairs and retreated to their vehicles. General Diego's assistant and guards were keeping their heads down, expecting an outburst of temper. His assistant knew he would need to remind the general about the promise to secure the release of the Russian bodyguard, but it would have to wait for the right moment.

As for General Diego, he knew the next day he would be in high-level negotiations with the Russians. He resolved not to let his error deter his focus.

Ambassador Montañez and Fernández looked at each other and exchanged a knowing smile. Costa and the chief went back into the station, as the chief remarked, "I don't know what just happened but we've never seen such powerful people come to our station and interfere in our affairs. I hope we never do again!" Then the chief put his hand on Costa's shoulder, comforting him, "You did a great job catching a fish. Don't be sad that somebody else let him off the hook."

Costa immediately checked with the airport. The charter plane had departed a half hour earlier and was well on the way to Cayman. He could try to secure Matvey there, but he remembered the ambassador's advice when he and Fernández had failed in Nassau: "I ask you to let this go. Return to your life in Cuba." Costa thought, "Yes, I will let this pass for now. But he better not show up in Cuba again!"

The Ritiki troupe charter plane touched down at the George Town airport. Matvey knew now that his past was in the past, as long as he never went back to Cuba. He turned to Clara, declaring, "We're finally here. This will be over soon, and we will be back at Callaloo Club and return to our normal lives. I've had some time to think. When we get back, there's a special place on Cat Island I want to take you to. It's a beautiful spot overlooking the island. You can see forever from the hilltop."

Clara smiled. Matvey said, "It seems I have been drifting with the tide for too long. Finally, my feet are on solid ground. The Bahamas is my home now."

If you enjoyed this book, learn more about Matvey's back story in

ACROSS FLORIDA STRAITS

follows a bastard son of a young Cuban dancer growing up in an all-inclusive Soviet resort on the south shore of Cuba. Matvey's larceny leads to entanglement with a traveling London art professor and his desperate need to escape Cuba. The story spans post-revolution life in Cuba through the Special Period and into modern times. His perilous journey takes him to Key West and a chance for a new life.

Other Books by Marvin Cook

HOUSEBOAT HERMIT OF THE EVERGLADES

Nefarious activities in the Everglades forge an unlikely friendship between Thompson, an old hermit living on a houseboat, and a burned-out and disillusioned National Park Service park ranger. Seeking a more peaceful wilderness and life changes, they migrate to North Florida's Nature Coast, encountering more adventures along the way.

CAN'T OUTRUN THE PAST

Enjoy the sequel to HOUSEBOAT HERMIT as trouble follows Thompson and Refuge Officer Bob Nelson, formerly a NPS Park Ranger, in North Florida's Big Bend wilderness. Unknown agents target Thompson to secure the secrets of his past only to be thwarted by the local sheriff and new friends.

DYSTOPIAN PARADISE

The story of Pilar, a young girl who is a force of nature, takes place in a future brought about by events occurring in modern times. Set in Florida and the Caribbean, Pilar ponders questions she cannot answer. What lies beyond the horizon?... Are we alone? When a ship appears in the distance her life takes a new path. In time, she discovers answers to some of her questions at Nueva Panacea.

THEY ALL CALLED HIM PINKY

Gold Award Winner, Florida Writers Association Royal Palm Literary Award

Written for children ages 8 and up, this book is illustrated with colorful images by Marvin Cook. The hero is a lone flamingo that visited St. Marks National Wildlife Refuge after a hurricane in 2018. Pinky makes new friends with many of the refuge's diverse bird species. The resident birds learn to accept Pinky, even though he is different. The story incorporates educational, moral and cultural lessons, with encouragement for kids to be the best they can be.